MYSTICONS™

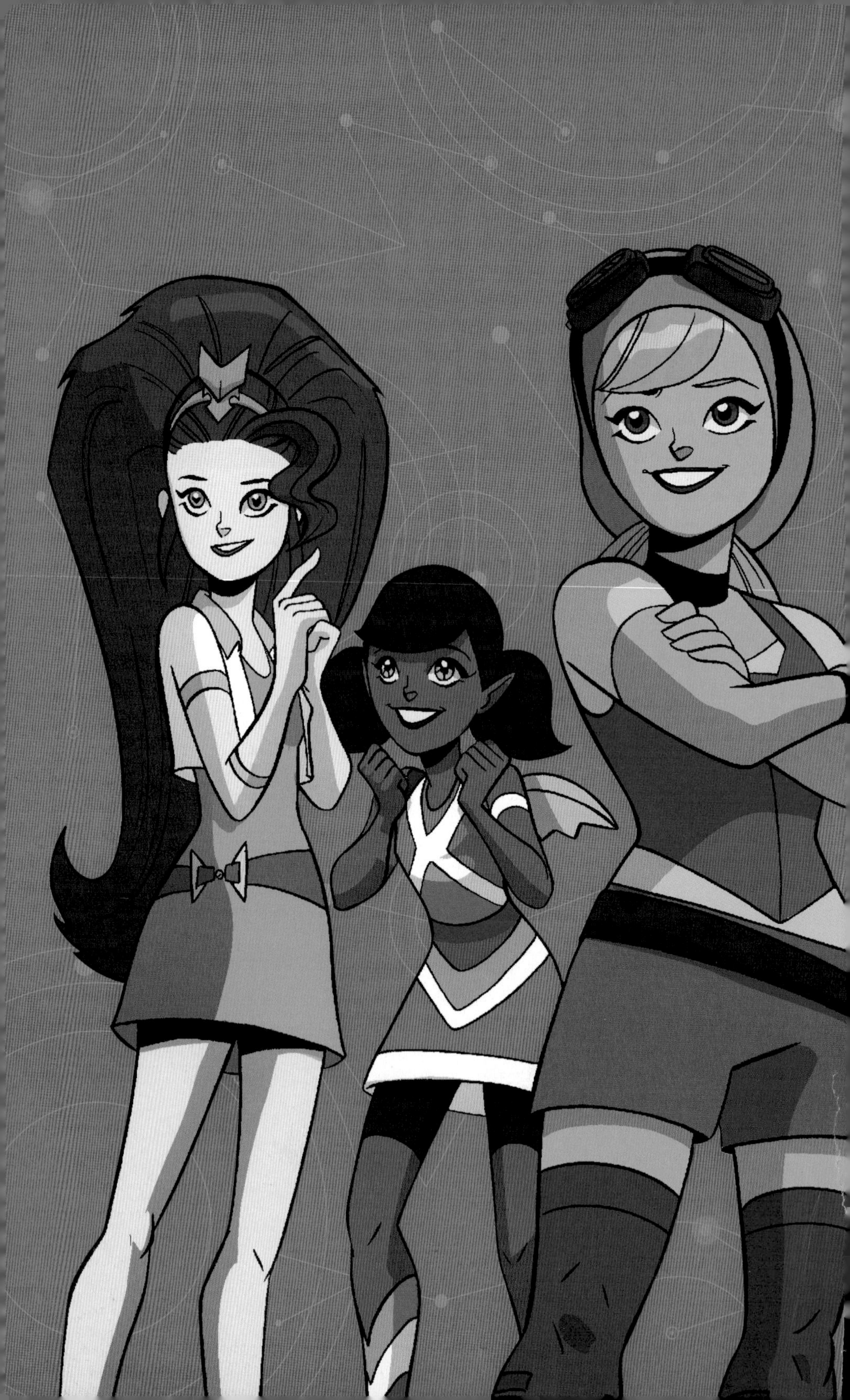

MYSTICONS™

VOLUME 2

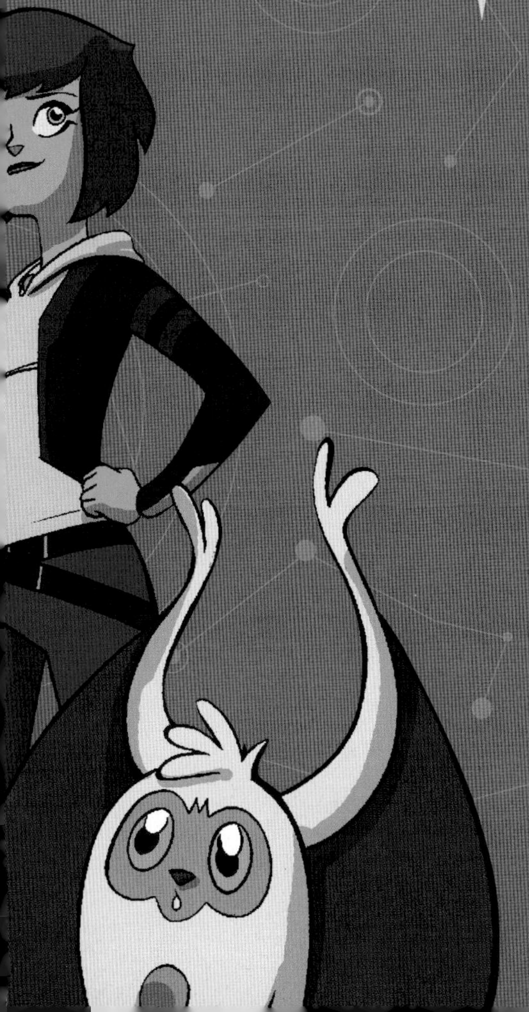

CREATED BY
SEAN JARA

STORY AND SCRIPT BY
KATE LETH

ART BY
MEGAN LEVENS

COLORS BY
MARISSA LOUISE

LETTERS BY
RACHEL DEERING

COVER BY
PAULINA GANUCHEAU

nelvana
DARK HORSE BOOKS

PRESIDENT AND PUBLISHER • MIKE RICHARDSON
EDITORS • SHANTEL LaROCQUE AND RACHEL ROBERTS
ASSISTANT EDITOR • BRETT ISRAEL
DESIGNER • SARAH TERRY
DIGITAL ART TECHNICIAN • JOSIE CHRISTENSEN

SPECIAL THANKS TO MARJANNE LYN, TALLY KNOLL, AND JEREMY KAPOSY.

Neil Hankerson Executive Vice President • Tom Weddle Chief Financial Officer • Randy Stradley Vice President
of Publishing • Nick McWhorter Chief Business Development Officer • Dale LaFountain Vice President of
Information Technology • Matt Parkinson Vice President of Marketing • Cara Niece Vice President of Production
and Scheduling • Mark Bernardi Vice President of Book Trade and Digital Sales • Ken Lizzi General Counsel
• Dave Marshall Editor in Chief • Davey Estrada Editorial Director • Chris Warner Senior Books Editor •
Cary Grazzini Director of Specialty Projects • Lia Ribacchi Art Director • Vanessa Todd-Holmes Director
of Print Purchasing • Matt Dryer Director of Digital Art and Prepress • Michael Gombos Senior Director of
Licensed Publishing • Kari Yadro Director of Custom Programs • Kari Torson Director of International Licensing

Published by Dark Horse Books
A division of Dark Horse Comics LLC
10956 SE Main Street, Milwaukie, OR 97222

First edition: May 2019 • ISBN 978-1-50670-876-8

10 9 8 7 6 5 4 3 2 1
Printed in China

To find a comics shop in your area, visit ComicShopLocator.com.

Library of Congress Cataloging-in-Publication Data

Names: Leth, Kate, author. | Jara, Sean, creator. | Levens, Megan, artist. |
  Louise, Marissa, colourist. | Piekos, Nate, letterer. | Bartel, Jen,
  artist. | Farrell, Triona, artist. | Deering, Rachel, 1983- letterer. |
  Ganucheau, Paulina, artist.
Title: Mysticons / created by Sean Jara ; story and script by Kate Leth ; art
  by Megan Levens ; colors by Marissa Louise ; letters by Nate Piekos of
  Blambot ; cover by Jen Bartel with Triona Farrell.
Description: First edition. | Milwaukie, OR : Dark Horse Books, 2018- | v. 2:
  letters by Rachel Deering ; cover by Paulina Ganucheau.
Identifiers: LCCN 2018008196| ISBN 9781506706474 (v. 1 : paperback) | ISBN
  9781506708768 (v. 2 : paperback)
Subjects: LCSH: Graphic novels. | BISAC: JUVENILE FICTION / Comics & Graphic
  Novels / Media Tie-In. | JUVENILE FICTION / Comics & Graphic Novels /
  Superheroes. | JUVENILE FICTION / Comics & Graphic Novels / General.
Classification: LCC PZ7.7.L48 My 2018 | DDC 741.5/973--dc23
LC record available at https://lccn.loc.gov/2018008196

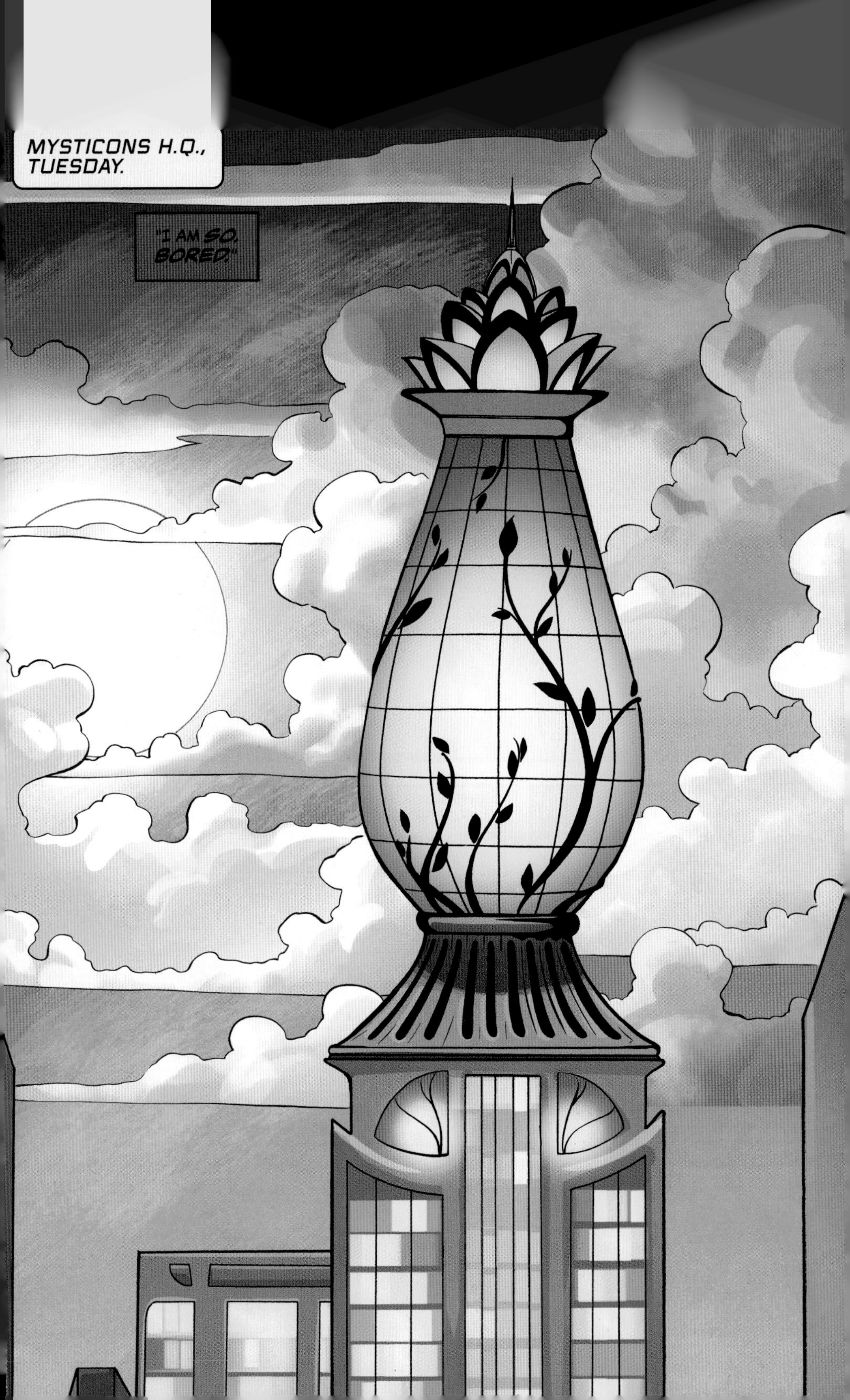
MYSTICONS H.Q., TUESDAY.
"I AM SO. BORED."

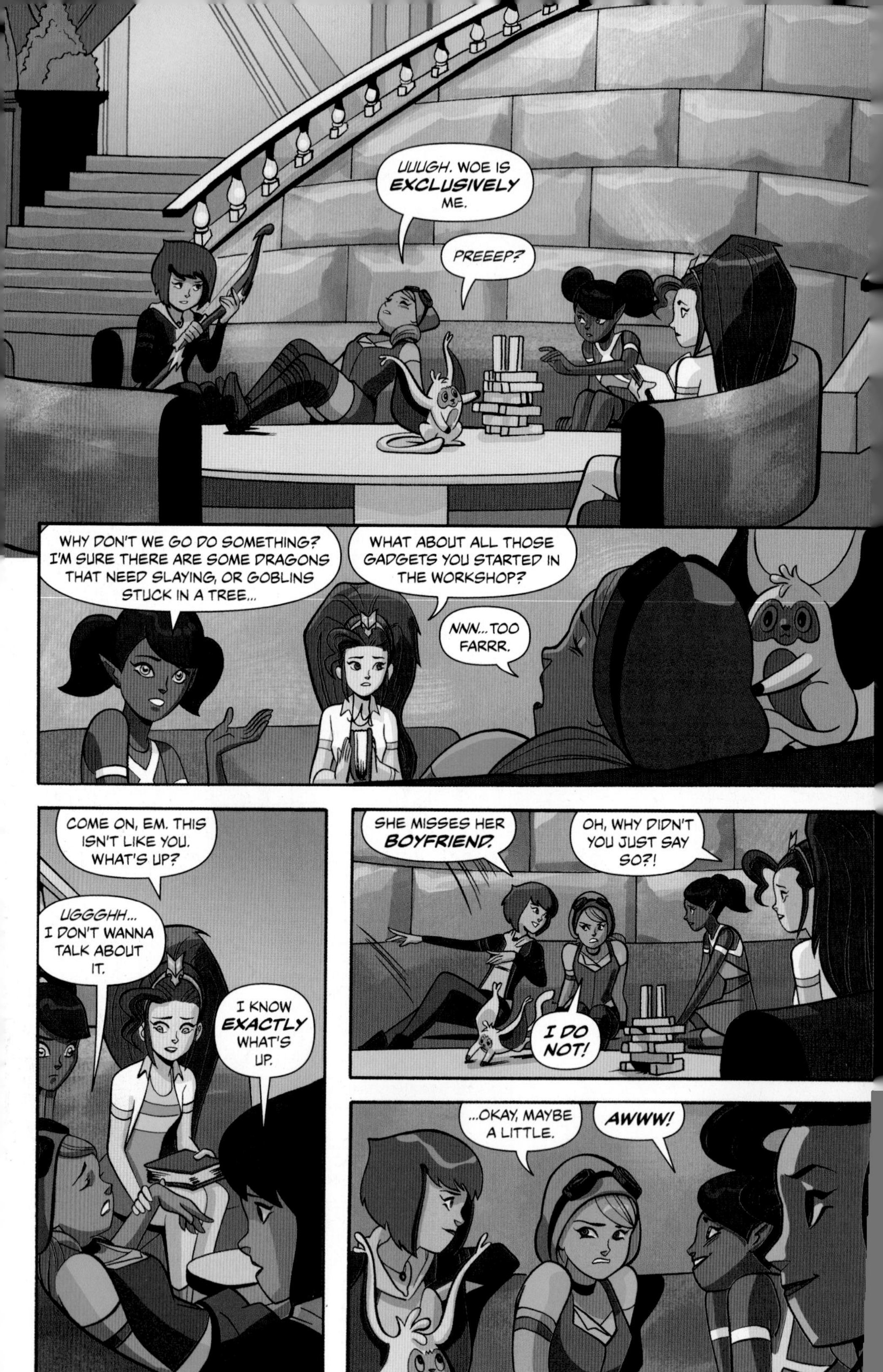
UUUGH. WOE IS **EXCLUSIVELY** ME.
PREEEP?
WHY DON'T WE GO DO SOMETHING? I'M SURE THERE ARE SOME DRAGONS THAT NEED SLAYING, OR GOBLINS STUCK IN A TREE...
WHAT ABOUT ALL THOSE GADGETS YOU STARTED IN THE WORKSHOP?
NNN... TOO FARRR.
COME ON, EM. THIS ISN'T LIKE YOU. WHAT'S UP?
UGGGHH... I DON'T WANNA TALK ABOUT IT.
I KNOW **EXACTLY** WHAT'S UP.
SHE MISSES HER **BOYFRIEND.**
OH, WHY DIDN'T YOU JUST SAY SO?!
I DO NOT!
...OKAY, MAYBE A LITTLE.
AWWW!

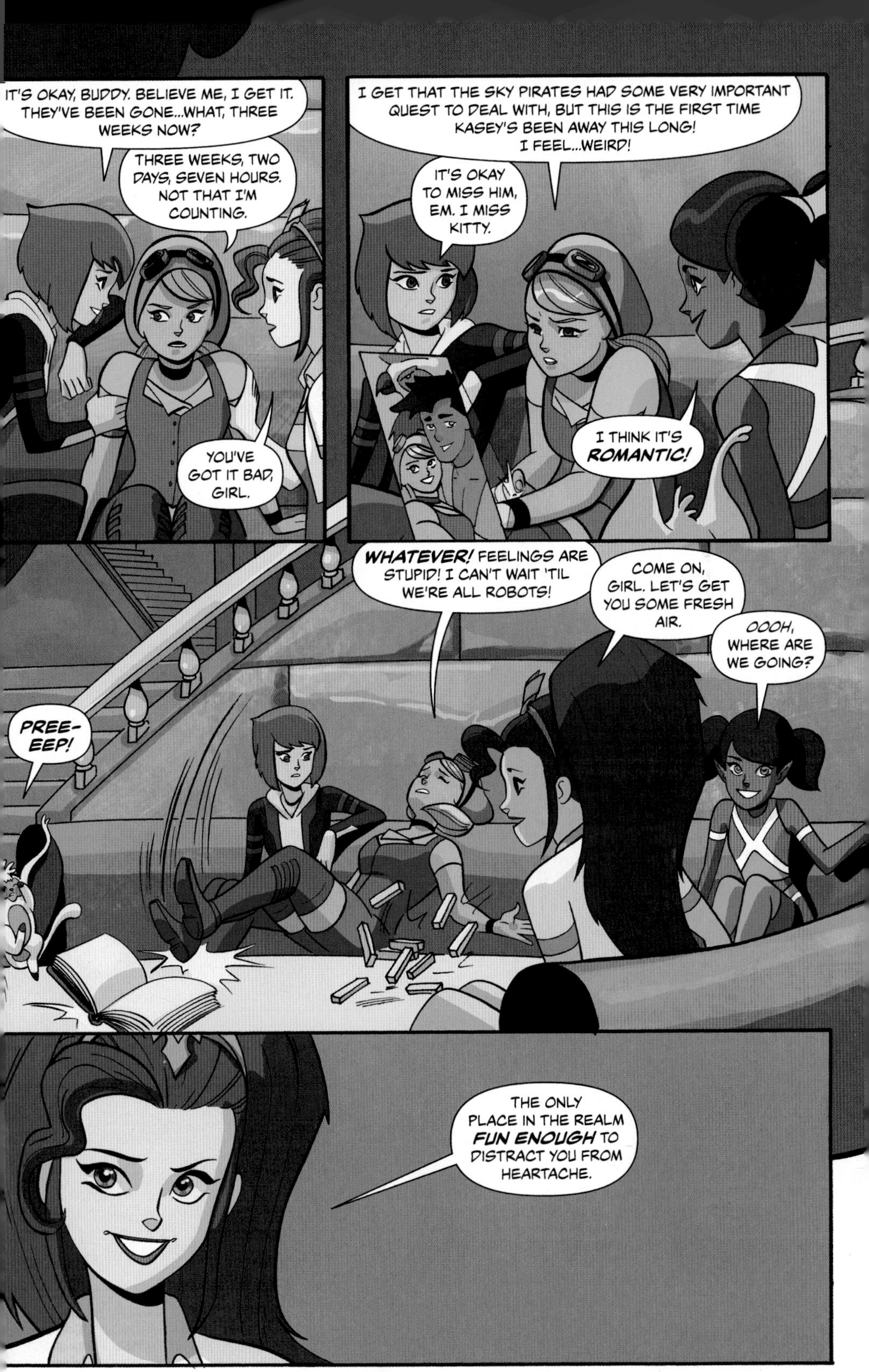

IT'S OKAY, BUDDY. BELIEVE ME, I GET IT. THEY'VE BEEN GONE...WHAT, THREE WEEKS NOW?
THREE WEEKS, TWO DAYS, SEVEN HOURS. NOT THAT I'M COUNTING.
YOU'VE GOT IT BAD, GIRL.
I GET THAT THE SKY PIRATES HAD SOME VERY IMPORTANT QUEST TO DEAL WITH, BUT THIS IS THE FIRST TIME KASEY'S BEEN AWAY THIS LONG! I FEEL...WEIRD!
IT'S OKAY TO MISS HIM, EM. I MISS KITTY.
I THINK IT'S ROMANTIC!
WHATEVER! FEELINGS ARE STUPID! I CAN'T WAIT 'TIL WE'RE ALL ROBOTS!
PREE-EEP!
COME ON, GIRL. LET'S GET YOU SOME FRESH AIR.
OOOH, WHERE ARE WE GOING?
THE ONLY PLACE IN THE REALM FUN ENOUGH TO DISTRACT YOU FROM HEARTACHE.

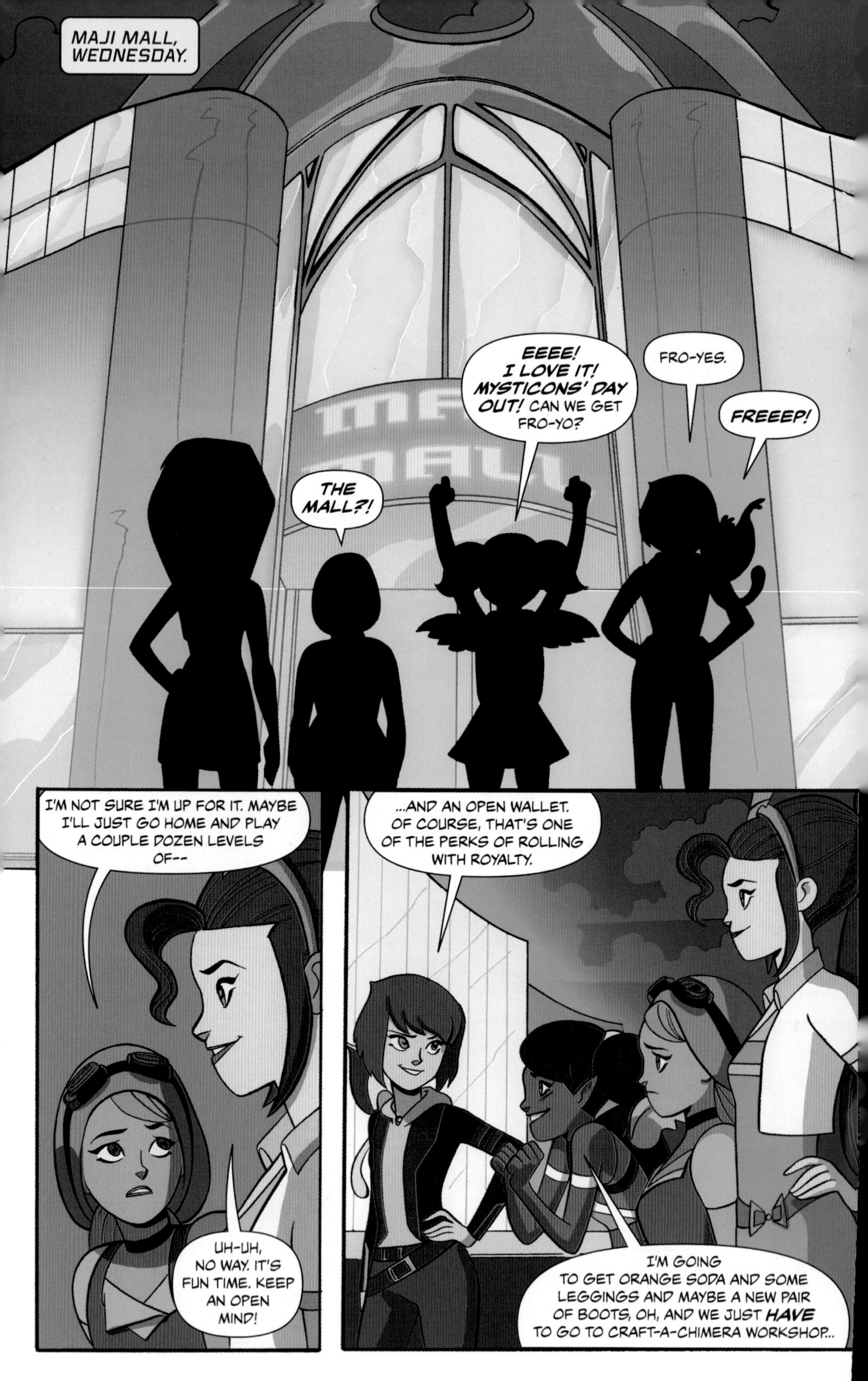
MAJI MALL, WEDNESDAY.
THE MALL?!
EEEE! I LOVE IT! MYSTICONS' DAY OUT! CAN WE GET FRO-YO?
FRO-YES.
FREEEP!
I'M NOT SURE I'M UP FOR IT. MAYBE I'LL JUST GO HOME AND PLAY A COUPLE DOZEN LEVELS OF--
UH-UH, NO WAY. IT'S FUN TIME. KEEP AN OPEN MIND!
...AND AN OPEN WALLET. OF COURSE, THAT'S ONE OF THE PERKS OF ROLLING WITH ROYALTY.
I'M GOING TO GET ORANGE SODA AND SOME LEGGINGS AND MAYBE A NEW PAIR OF BOOTS, OH, AND WE JUST HAVE TO GO TO CRAFT-A-CHIMERA WORKSHOP...

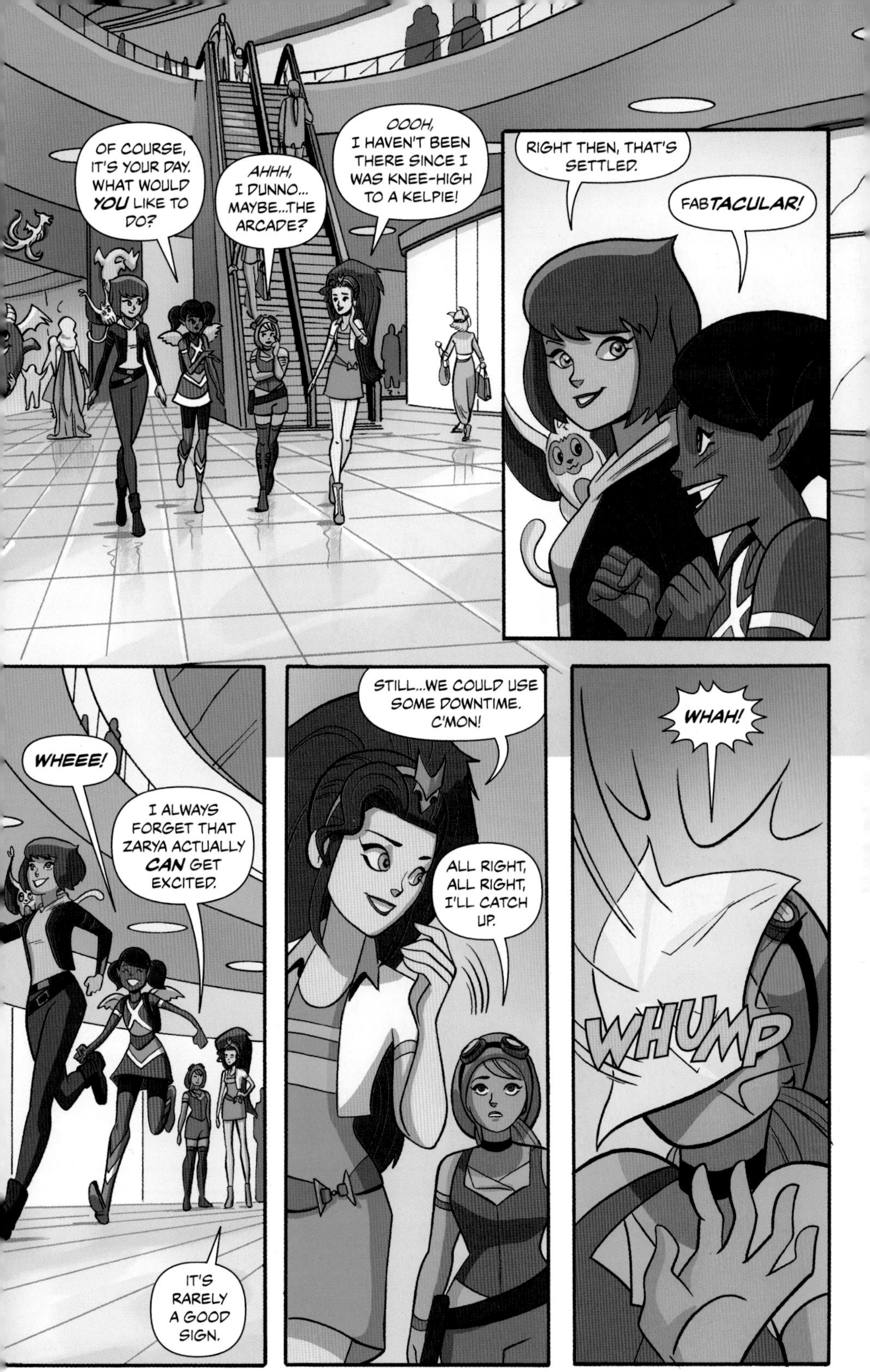
OF COURSE, IT'S YOUR DAY. WHAT WOULD YOU LIKE TO DO?
AHHH, I DUNNO... MAYBE...THE ARCADE?
OOOH, I HAVEN'T BEEN THERE SINCE I WAS KNEE-HIGH TO A KELPIE!
RIGHT THEN, THAT'S SETTLED.
FABTACULAR!
WHEEE!
I ALWAYS FORGET THAT ZARYA ACTUALLY CAN GET EXCITED.
IT'S RARELY A GOOD SIGN.
STILL...WE COULD USE SOME DOWNTIME. C'MON!
ALL RIGHT, ALL RIGHT, I'LL CATCH UP.
WHAH!
WHUMP

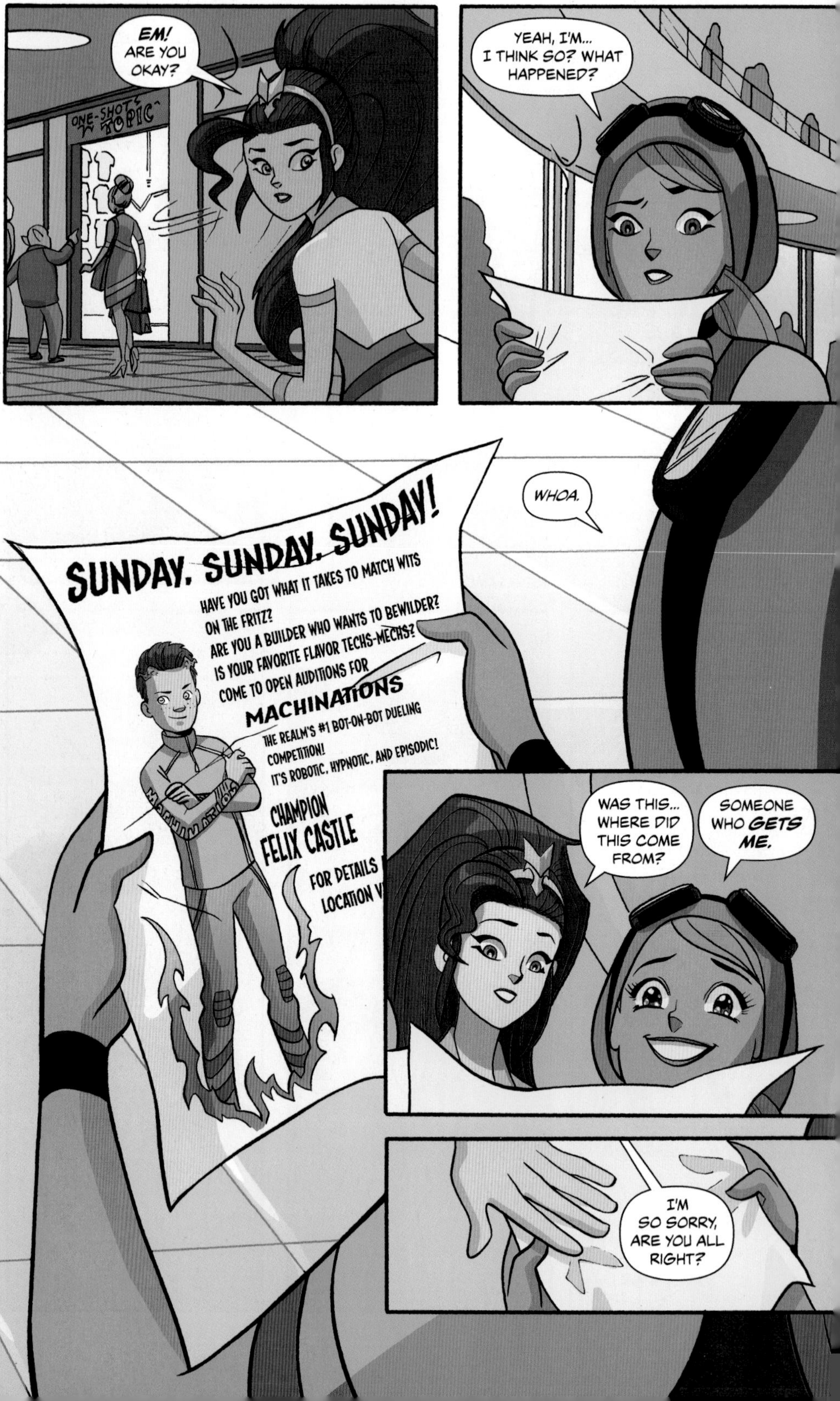

EM! ARE YOU OKAY?
ONE-SHOT TOPIC
YEAH, I'M... I THINK SO? WHAT HAPPENED?
WHOA.
SUNDAY. SUNDAY. SUNDAY!
HAVE YOU GOT WHAT IT TAKES TO MATCH WITS ON THE FRITZ?
ARE YOU A BUILDER WHO WANTS TO BEWILDER?
IS YOUR FAVORITE FLAVOR TECHS-MECHS?
COME TO OPEN AUDITIONS FOR
MACHINATIONS
THE REALM'S #1 BOT-ON-BOT DUELING COMPETITION!
IT'S ROBOTIC, HYPNOTIC, AND EPISODIC!
CHAMPION
FELIX CASTLE
FOR DETAILS
LOCATION V
WAS THIS... WHERE DID THIS COME FROM?
SOMEONE WHO *GETS* *ME.*
I'M SO SORRY, ARE YOU ALL RIGHT?

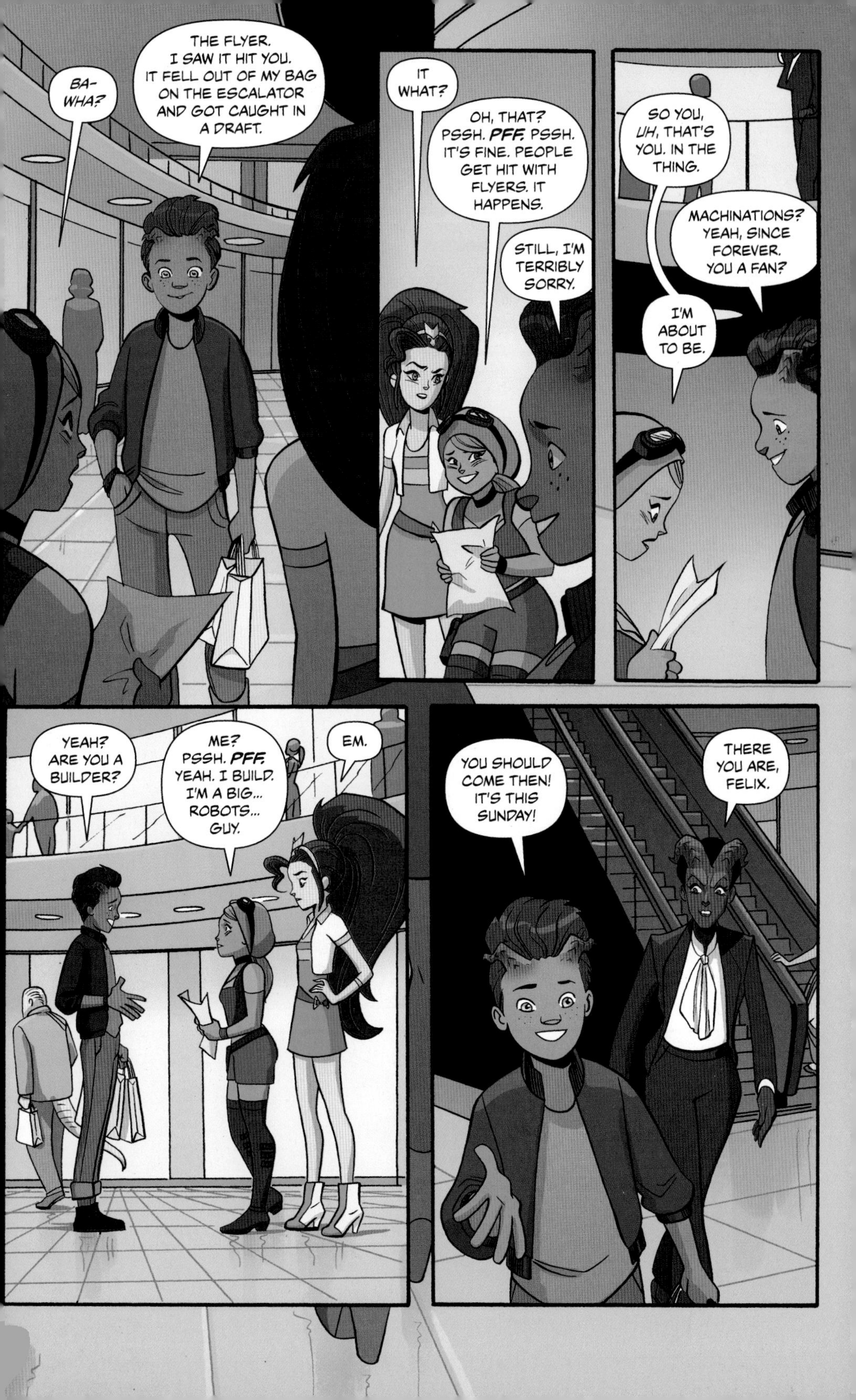
BA-WHA?
THE FLYER. I SAW IT HIT YOU. IT FELL OUT OF MY BAG ON THE ESCALATOR AND GOT CAUGHT IN A DRAFT.
IT WHAT?
OH, THAT? PSSH. PFF. PSSH. IT'S FINE. PEOPLE GET HIT WITH FLYERS. IT HAPPENS.
STILL, I'M TERRIBLY SORRY.
SO YOU, UH, THAT'S YOU. IN THE THING.
MACHINATIONS? YEAH, SINCE FOREVER. YOU A FAN?
I'M ABOUT TO BE.
YEAH? ARE YOU A BUILDER?
ME? PSSH. PFF. YEAH. I BUILD. I'M A BIG... ROBOTS... GUY.
EM.
YOU SHOULD COME THEN! IT'S THIS SUNDAY!
THERE YOU ARE, FELIX.

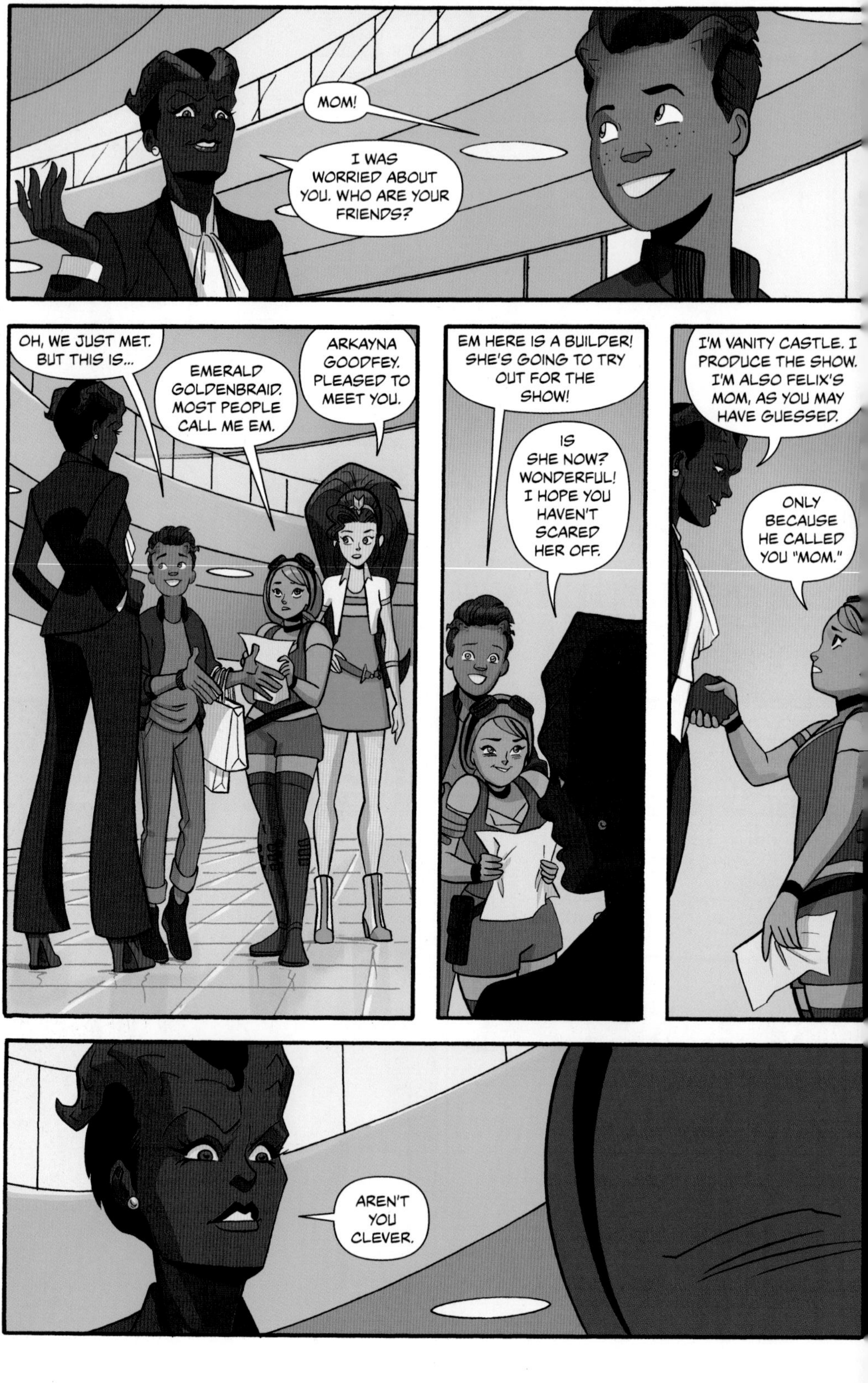
MOM!
I WAS WORRIED ABOUT YOU. WHO ARE YOUR FRIENDS?
OH, WE JUST MET. BUT THIS IS...
EMERALD GOLDENBRAID. MOST PEOPLE CALL ME EM.
ARKAYNA GOODFEY. PLEASED TO MEET YOU.
EM HERE IS A BUILDER! SHE'S GOING TO TRY OUT FOR THE SHOW!
IS SHE NOW? WONDERFUL! I HOPE YOU HAVEN'T SCARED HER OFF.
I'M VANITY CASTLE. I PRODUCE THE SHOW. I'M ALSO FELIX'S MOM, AS YOU MAY HAVE GUESSED.
ONLY BECAUSE HE CALLED YOU "MOM."
AREN'T YOU CLEVER.

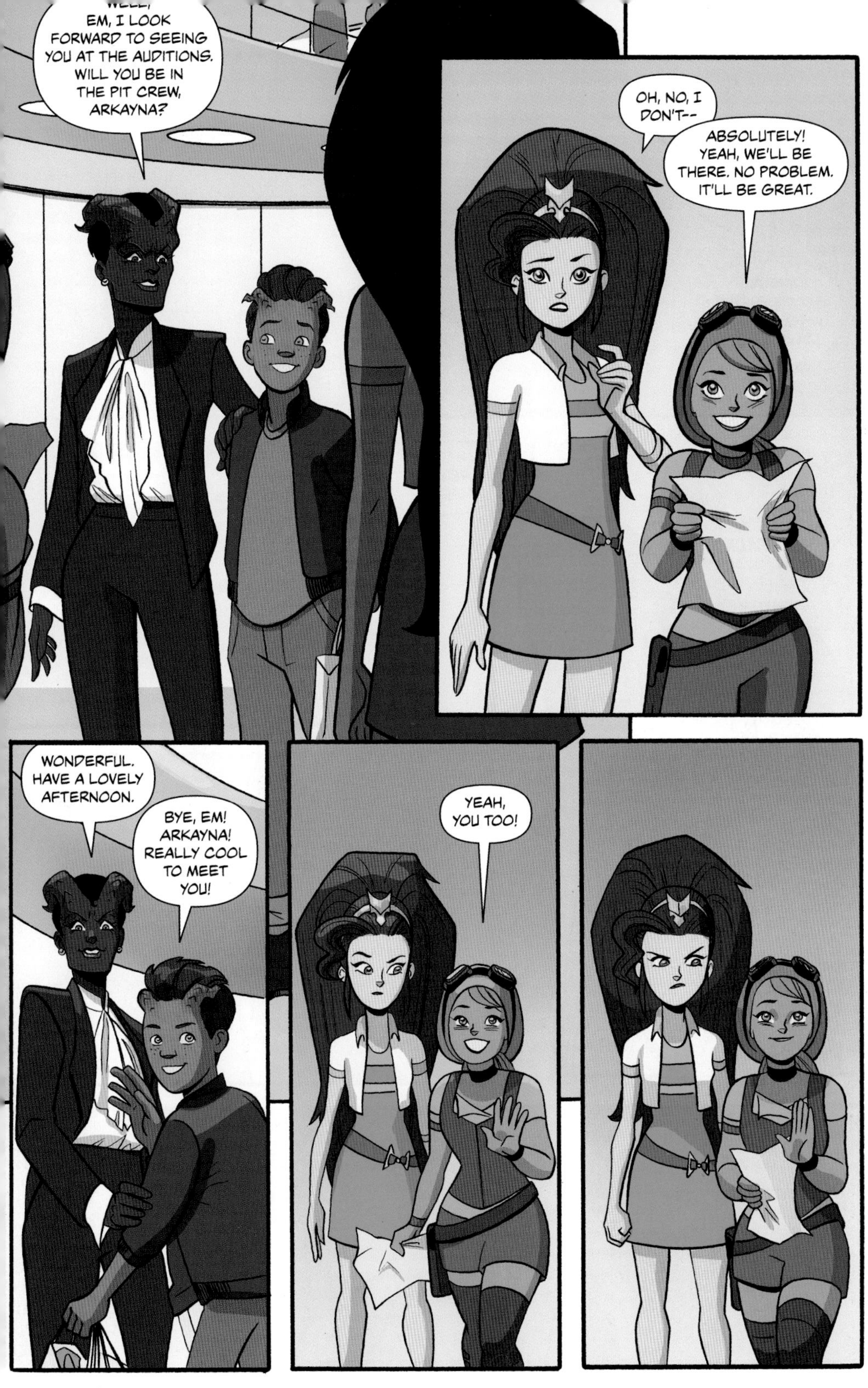
EM, I LOOK FORWARD TO SEEING YOU AT THE AUDITIONS. WILL YOU BE IN THE PIT CREW, ARKAYNA?
OH, NO, I DON'T--
ABSOLUTELY! YEAH, WE'LL BE THERE. NO PROBLEM. IT'LL BE GREAT.
WONDERFUL. HAVE A LOVELY AFTERNOON.
BYE, EM! ARKAYNA! REALLY COOL TO MEET YOU!
YEAH, YOU TOO!

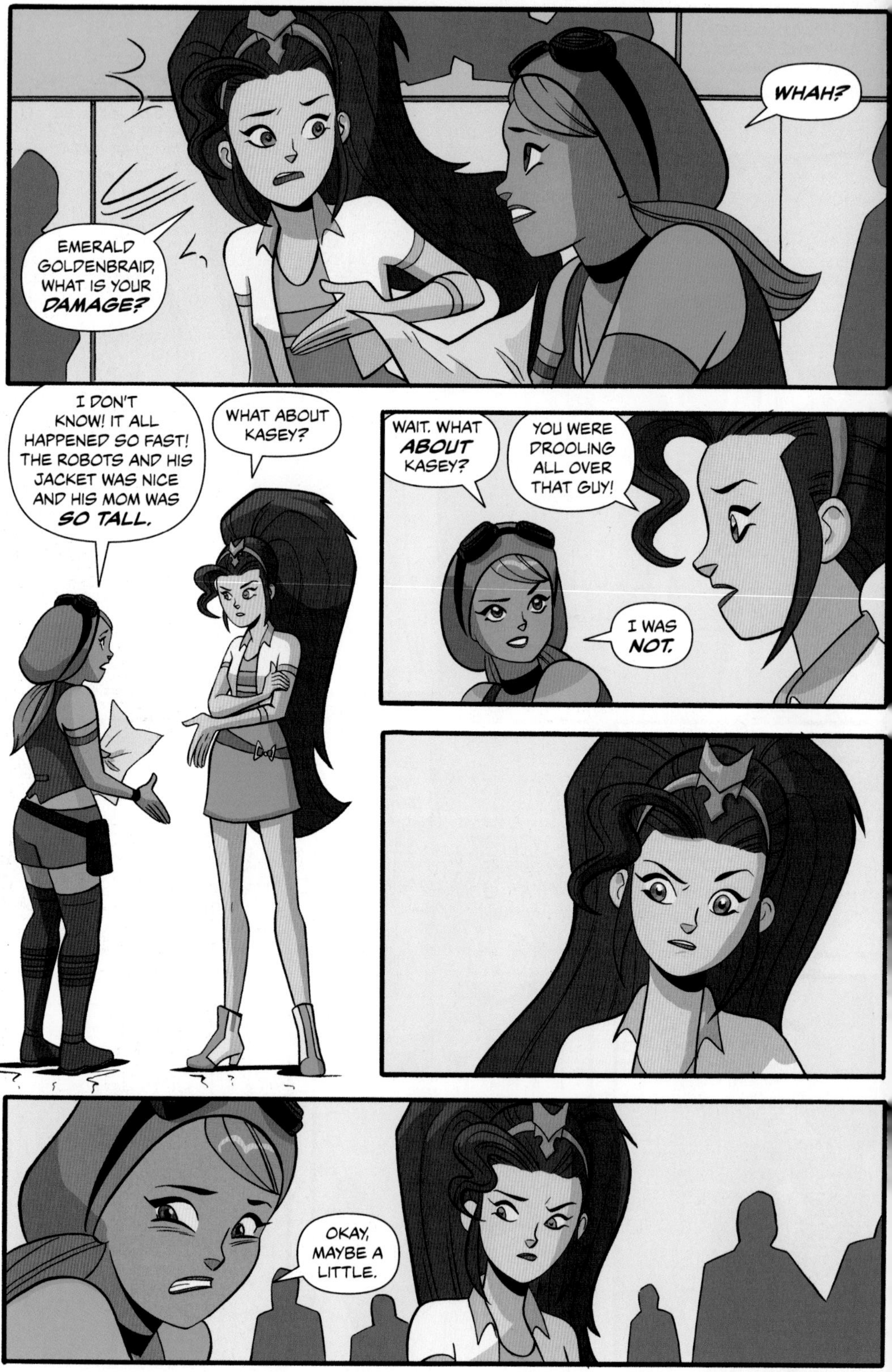
WHAH?
EMERALD GOLDENBRAID, WHAT IS YOUR DAMAGE?
I DON'T KNOW! IT ALL HAPPENED SO FAST! THE ROBOTS AND HIS JACKET WAS NICE AND HIS MOM WAS SO TALL.
WHAT ABOUT KASEY?
WAIT. WHAT ABOUT KASEY?
YOU WERE DROOLING ALL OVER THAT GUY!
I WAS NOT.
OKAY, MAYBE A LITTLE.

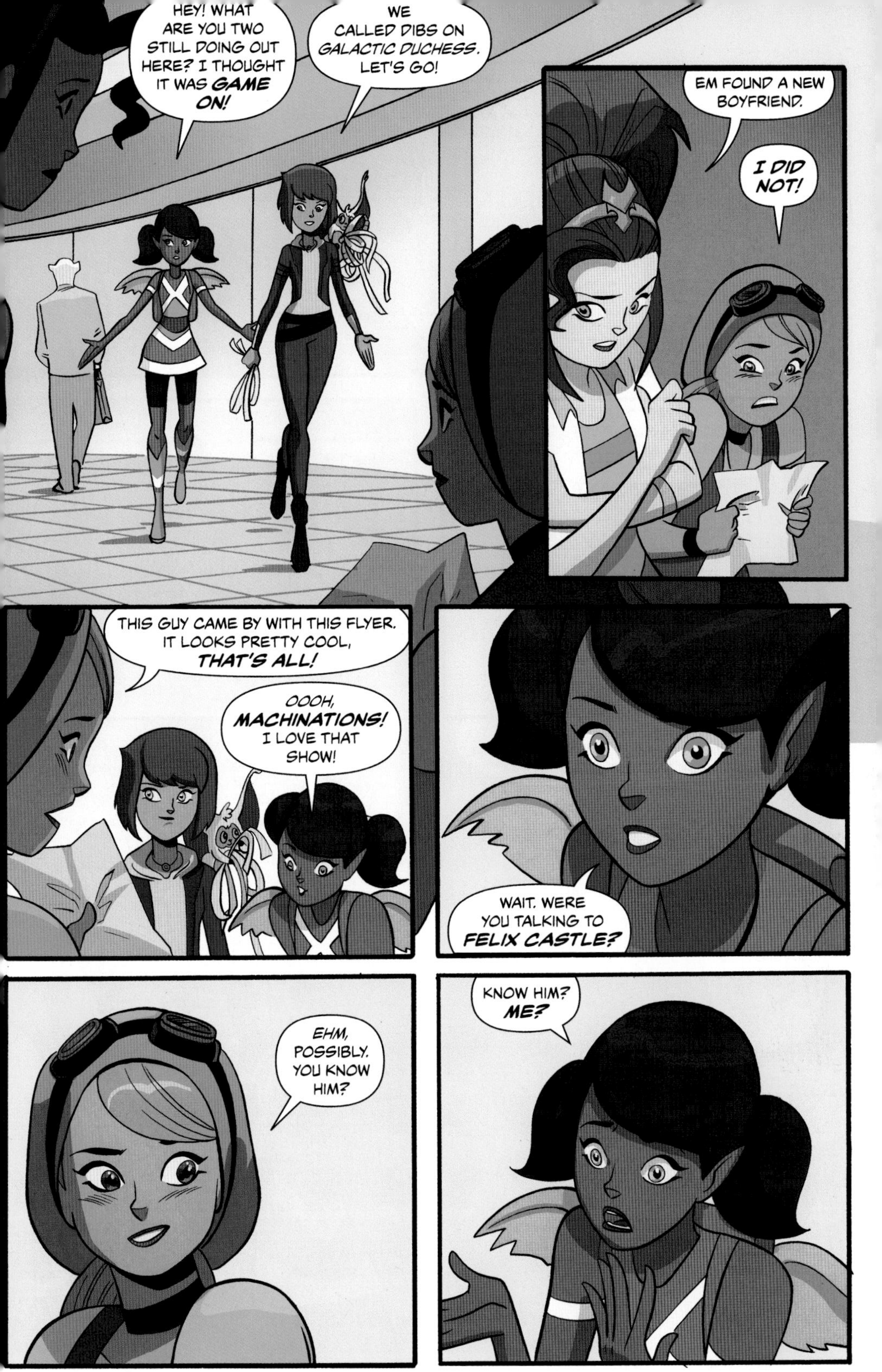

HEY! WHAT ARE YOU TWO STILL DOING OUT HERE? I THOUGHT IT WAS **GAME ON!**
WE CALLED DIBS ON *GALACTIC DUCHESS*. LET'S GO!
EM FOUND A NEW BOYFRIEND.
I DID NOT!
THIS GUY CAME BY WITH THIS FLYER. IT LOOKS PRETTY COOL, **THAT'S ALL!**
OOOH, **MACHINATIONS!** I LOVE THAT SHOW!
WAIT. WERE YOU TALKING TO **FELIX CASTLE?**
EHM, POSSIBLY. YOU KNOW HIM?
KNOW HIM? **ME?**

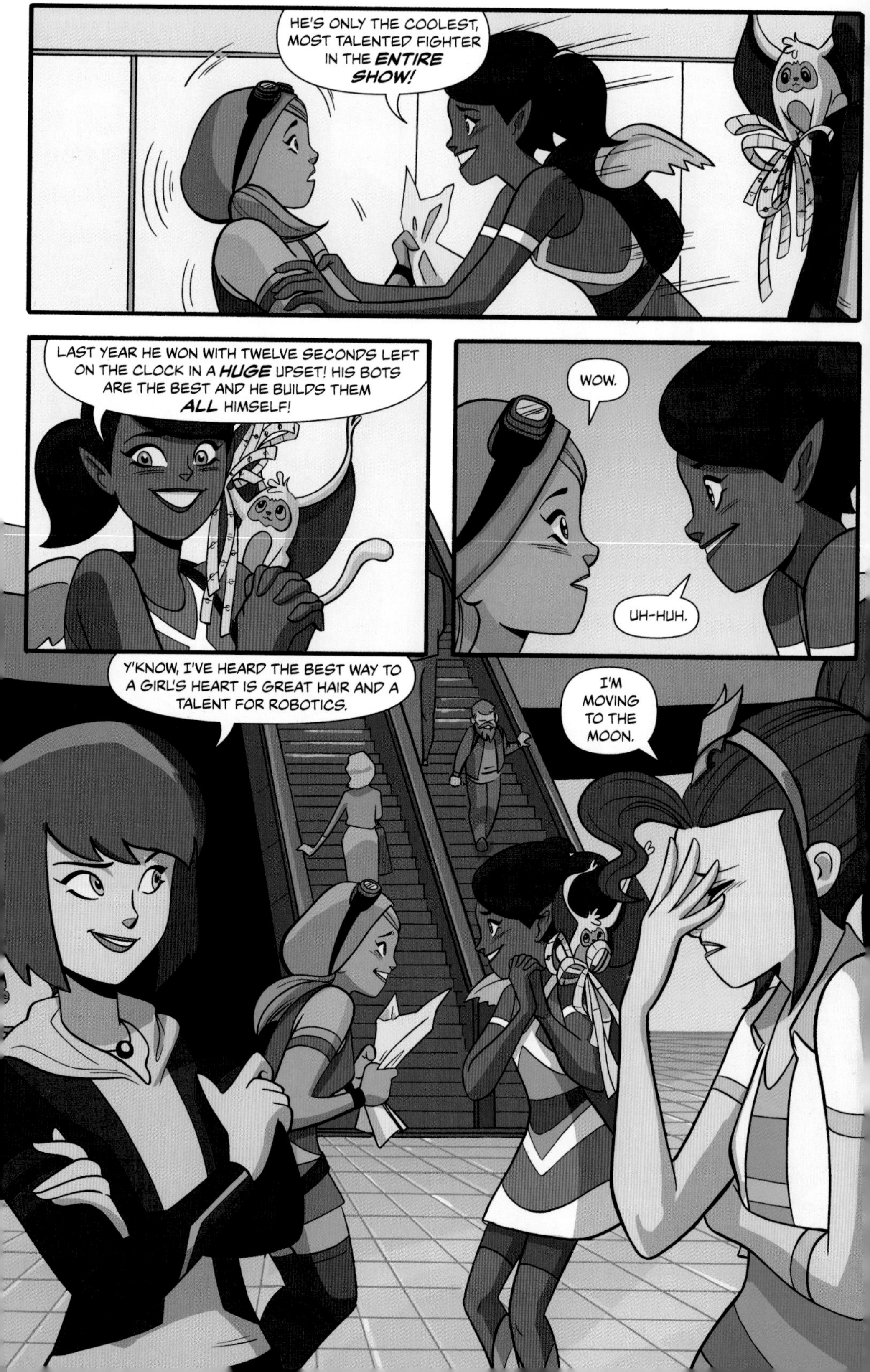
HE'S ONLY THE COOLEST, MOST TALENTED FIGHTER IN THE ENTIRE SHOW!
LAST YEAR HE WON WITH TWELVE SECONDS LEFT ON THE CLOCK IN A HUGE UPSET! HIS BOTS ARE THE BEST AND HE BUILDS THEM ALL HIMSELF!
WOW.
UH-HUH.
Y'KNOW, I'VE HEARD THE BEST WAY TO A GIRL'S HEART IS GREAT HAIR AND A TALENT FOR ROBOTICS.
I'M MOVING TO THE MOON.

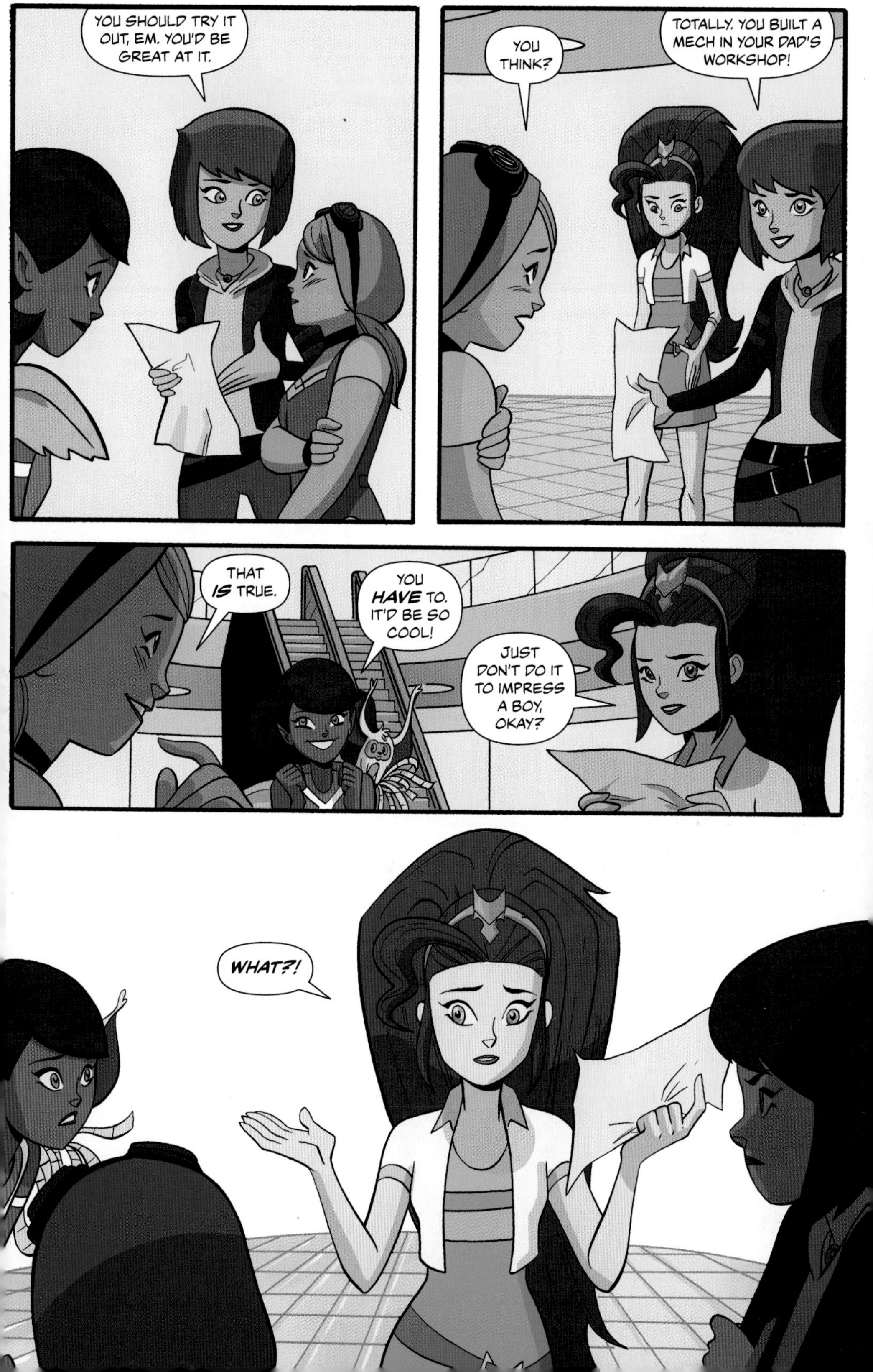

YOU SHOULD TRY IT OUT, EM. YOU'D BE GREAT AT IT.
YOU THINK?
TOTALLY. YOU BUILT A MECH IN YOUR DAD'S WORKSHOP!
THAT IS TRUE.
YOU HAVE TO. IT'D BE SO COOL!
JUST DON'T DO IT TO IMPRESS A BOY, OKAY?
WHAT?!

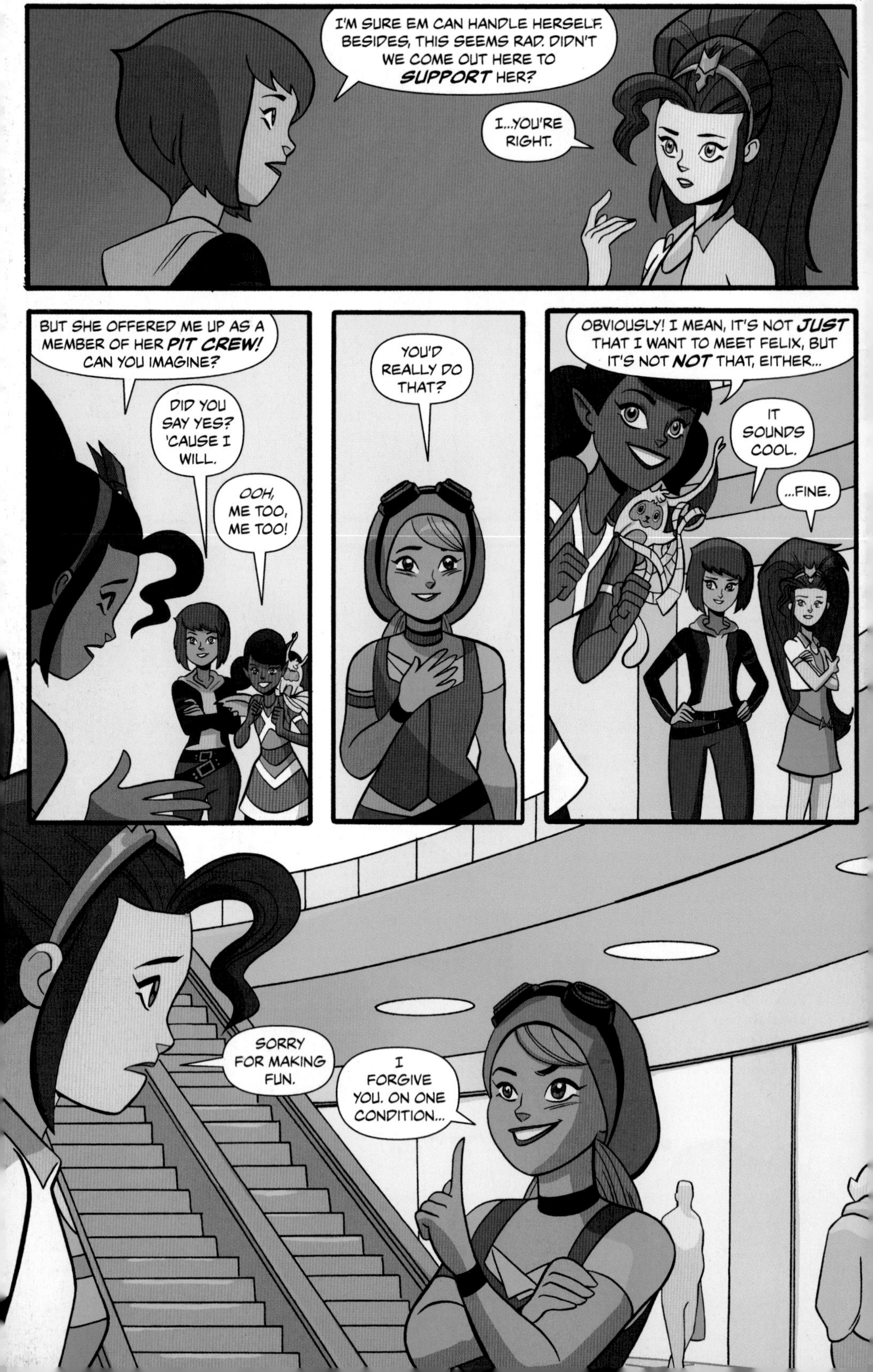
I'M SURE EM CAN HANDLE HERSELF. BESIDES, THIS SEEMS RAD. DIDN'T WE COME OUT HERE TO SUPPORT HER?
I...YOU'RE RIGHT.
BUT SHE OFFERED ME UP AS A MEMBER OF HER PIT CREW! CAN YOU IMAGINE?
DID YOU SAY YES? 'CAUSE I WILL.
OOH, ME TOO, ME TOO!
YOU'D REALLY DO THAT?
OBVIOUSLY! I MEAN, IT'S NOT JUST THAT I WANT TO MEET FELIX, BUT IT'S NOT NOT THAT, EITHER...
IT SOUNDS COOL.
...FINE.
SORRY FOR MAKING FUN.
I FORGIVE YOU. ON ONE CONDITION...

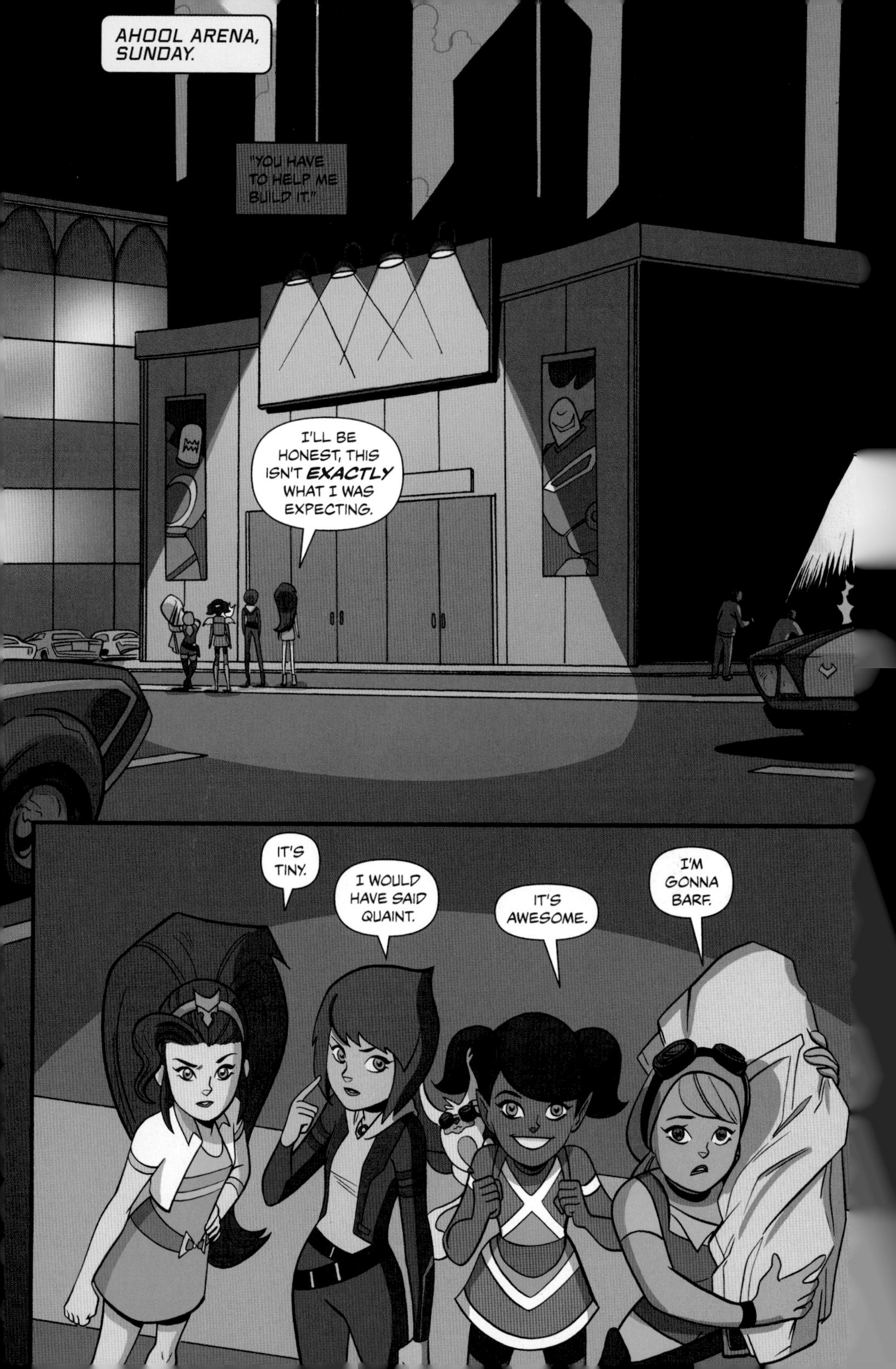
AHOOL ARENA, SUNDAY.
"YOU HAVE TO HELP ME BUILD IT."
I'LL BE HONEST, THIS ISN'T EXACTLY WHAT I WAS EXPECTING.
IT'S TINY.
I WOULD HAVE SAID QUAINT.
IT'S AWESOME.
I'M GONNA BARF.

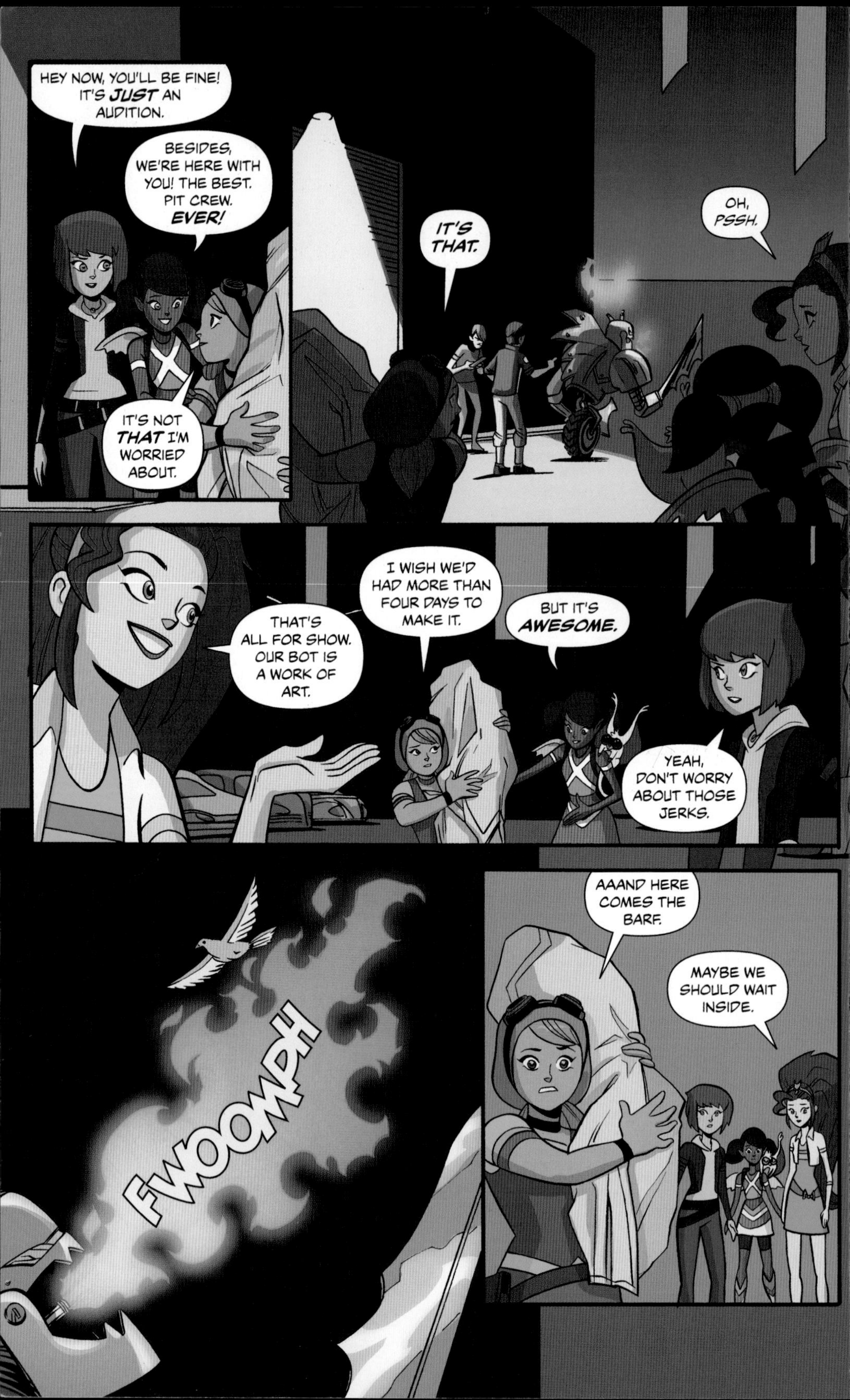
HEY NOW, YOU'LL BE FINE! IT'S JUST AN AUDITION.
BESIDES, WE'RE HERE WITH YOU! THE BEST. PIT CREW. EVER!
IT'S NOT THAT I'M WORRIED ABOUT.
IT'S THAT.
OH, PSSH.
THAT'S ALL FOR SHOW. OUR BOT IS A WORK OF ART.
I WISH WE'D HAD MORE THAN FOUR DAYS TO MAKE IT.
BUT IT'S AWESOME.
YEAH, DON'T WORRY ABOUT THOSE JERKS.
FWOOMPH
AAAND HERE COMES THE BARF.
MAYBE WE SHOULD WAIT INSIDE.

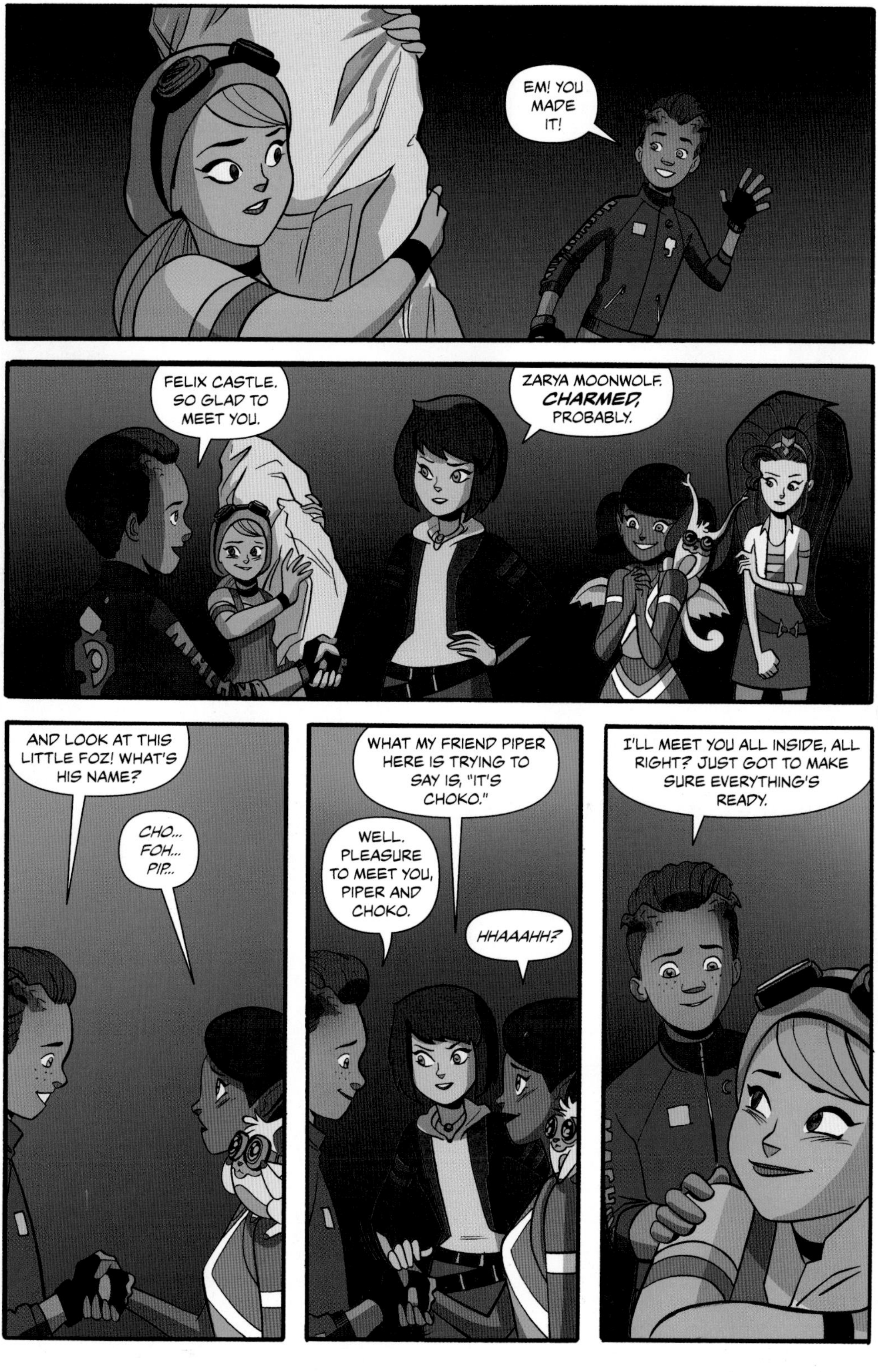
EM! YOU MADE IT!
FELIX CASTLE. SO GLAD TO MEET YOU.
ZARYA MOONWOLF. CHARMED, PROBABLY.
AND LOOK AT THIS LITTLE FOZ! WHAT'S HIS NAME?
CHO... FOH... PIP...
WHAT MY FRIEND PIPER HERE IS TRYING TO SAY IS, "IT'S CHOKO."
WELL. PLEASURE TO MEET YOU, PIPER AND CHOKO.
HHAAAHH?
I'LL MEET YOU ALL INSIDE, ALL RIGHT? JUST GOT TO MAKE SURE EVERYTHING'S READY.

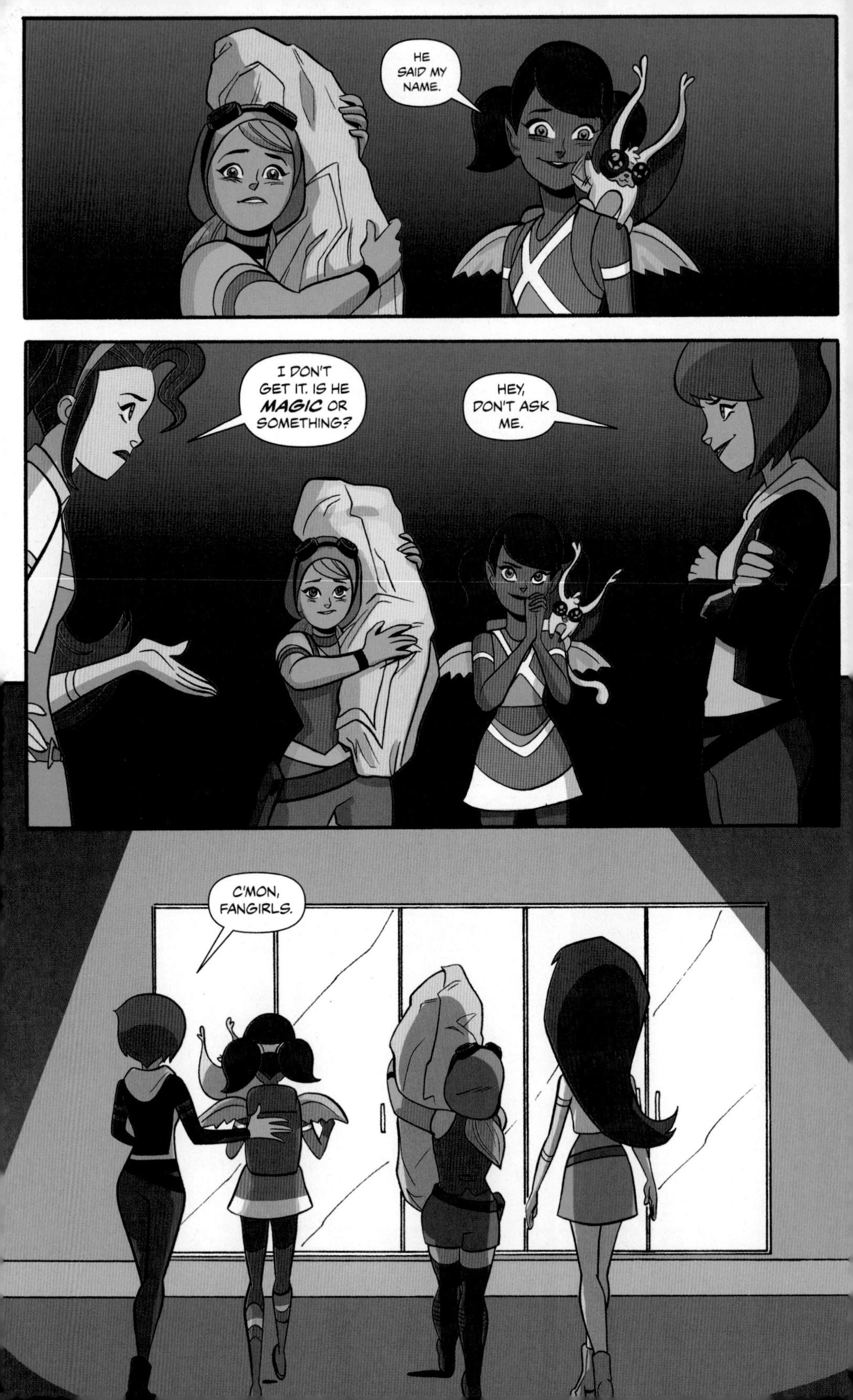
HE SAID MY NAME.
I DON'T GET IT. IS HE MAGIC OR SOMETHING?
HEY, DON'T ASK ME.
C'MON, FANGIRLS.

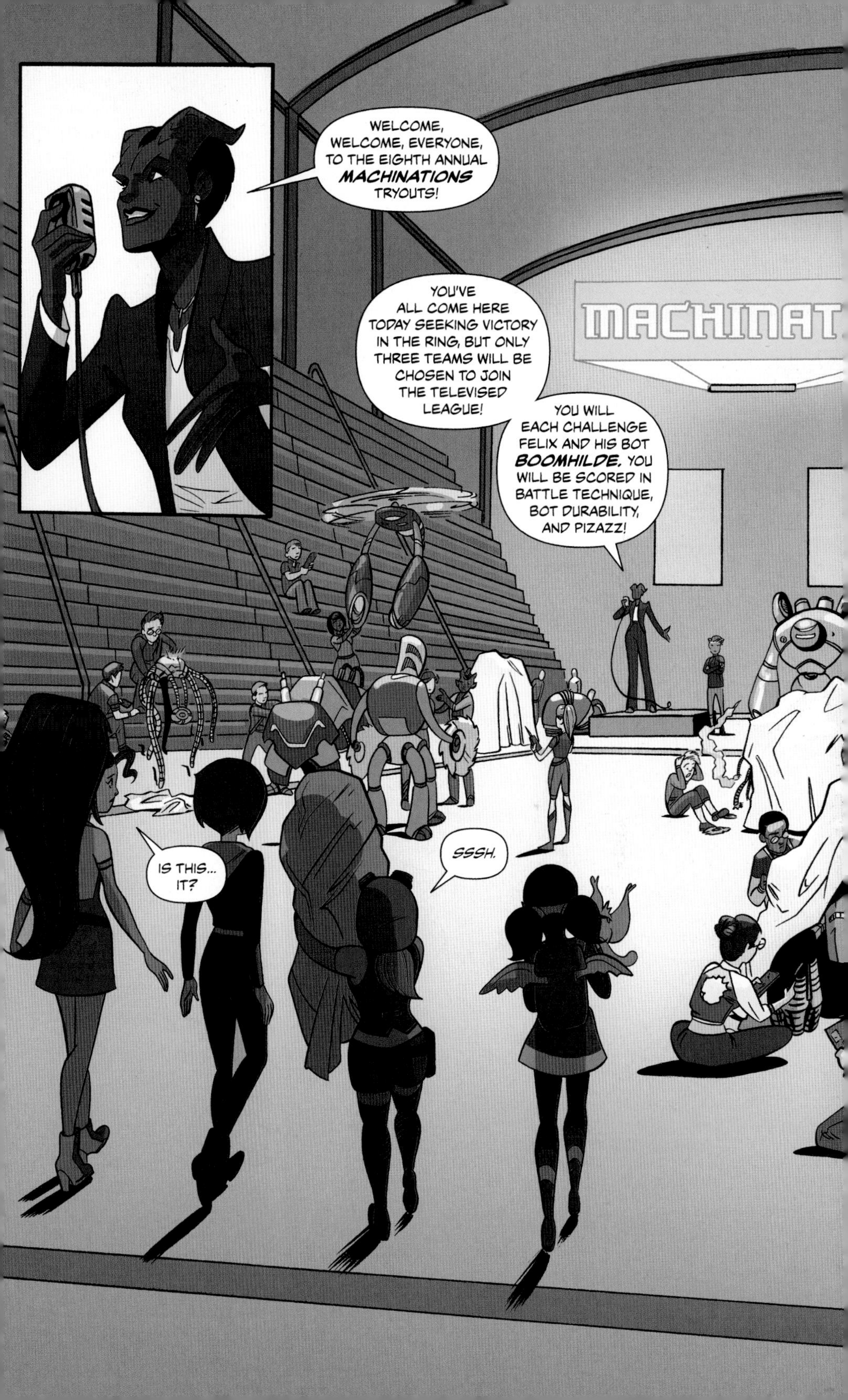
WELCOME, WELCOME, EVERYONE, TO THE EIGHTH ANNUAL MACHINATIONS TRYOUTS!
YOU'VE ALL COME HERE TODAY SEEKING VICTORY IN THE RING, BUT ONLY THREE TEAMS WILL BE CHOSEN TO JOIN THE TELEVISED LEAGUE!
YOU WILL EACH CHALLENGE FELIX AND HIS BOT BOOMHILDE. YOU WILL BE SCORED IN BATTLE TECHNIQUE, BOT DURABILITY, AND PIZAZZ!
IS THIS... IT?
SSSH.

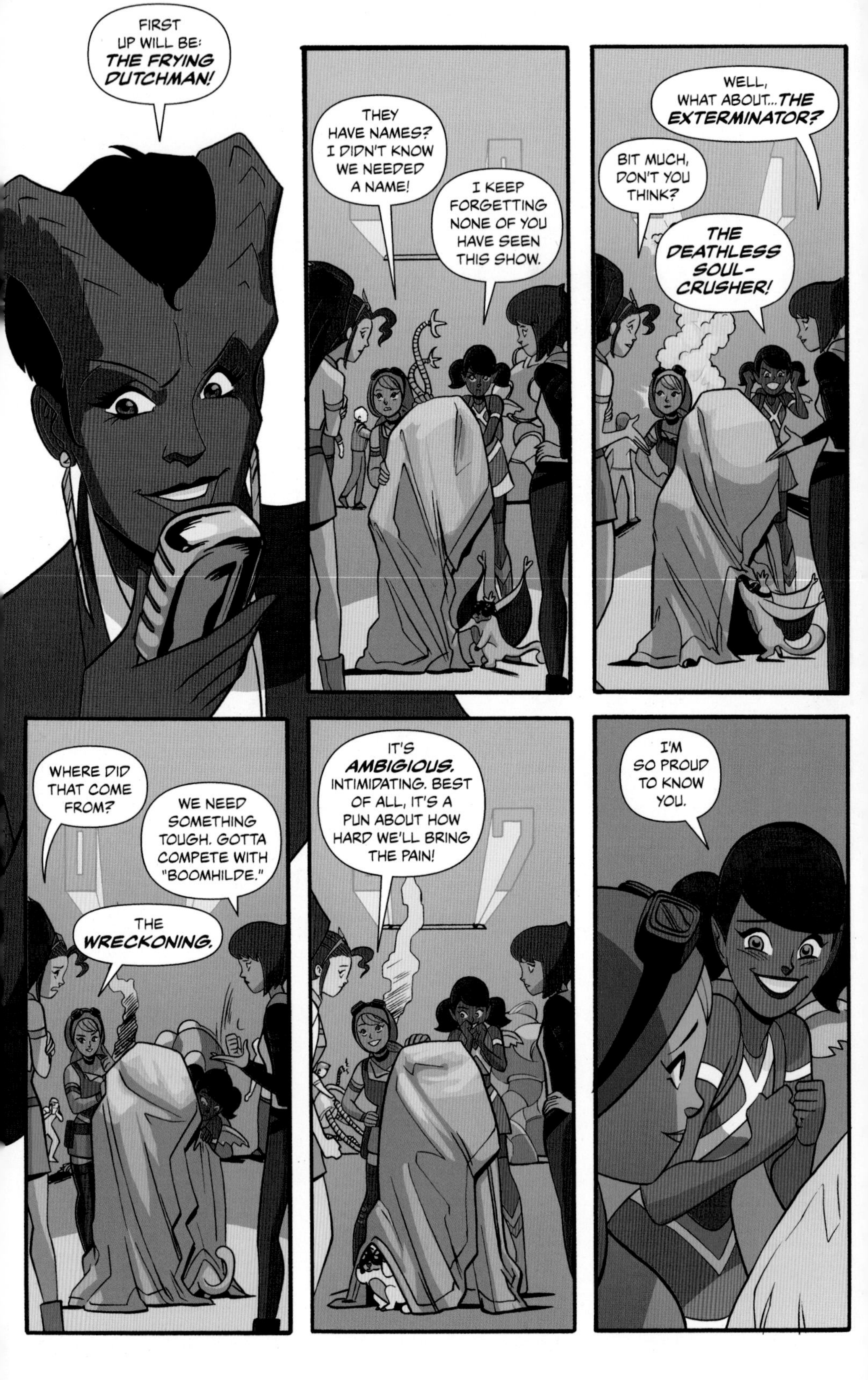
FIRST UP WILL BE: THE FRYING DUTCHMAN!
THEY HAVE NAMES? I DIDN'T KNOW WE NEEDED A NAME!
I KEEP FORGETTING NONE OF YOU HAVE SEEN THIS SHOW.
WELL, WHAT ABOUT...THE EXTERMINATOR?
BIT MUCH, DON'T YOU THINK?
THE DEATHLESS SOUL-CRUSHER!
WHERE DID THAT COME FROM?
WE NEED SOMETHING TOUGH. GOTTA COMPETE WITH "BOOMHILDE."
THE WRECKONING.
IT'S AMBIGIOUS. INTIMIDATING. BEST OF ALL, IT'S A PUN ABOUT HOW HARD WE'LL BRING THE PAIN!
I'M SO PROUD TO KNOW YOU.

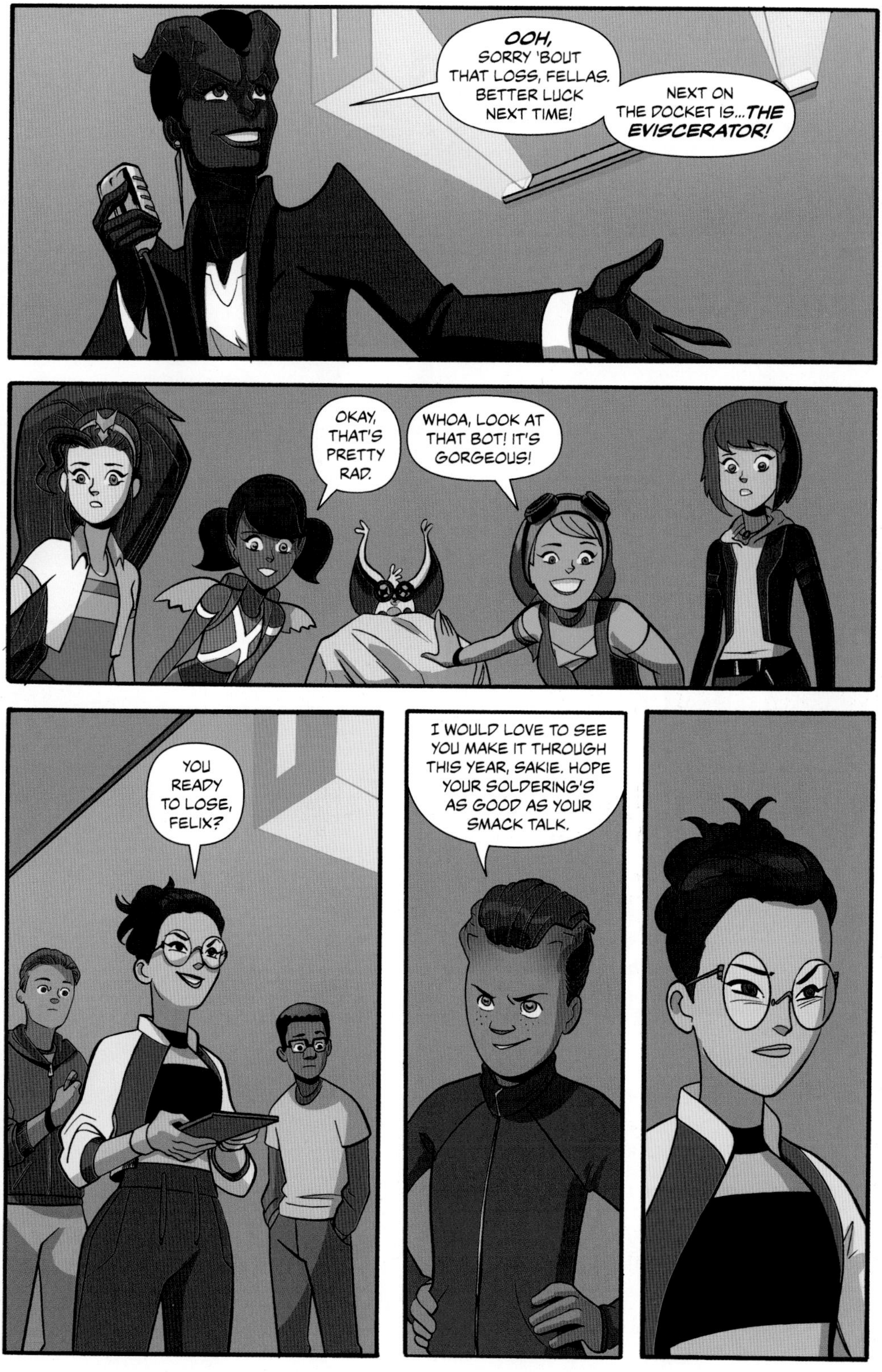
OOH, SORRY 'BOUT THAT LOSS, FELLAS. BETTER LUCK NEXT TIME!
NEXT ON THE DOCKET IS...THE EVISCERATOR!
OKAY, THAT'S PRETTY RAD.
WHOA, LOOK AT THAT BOT! IT'S GORGEOUS!
YOU READY TO LOSE, FELIX?
I WOULD LOVE TO SEE YOU MAKE IT THROUGH THIS YEAR, SAKIE. HOPE YOUR SOLDERING'S AS GOOD AS YOUR SMACK TALK.

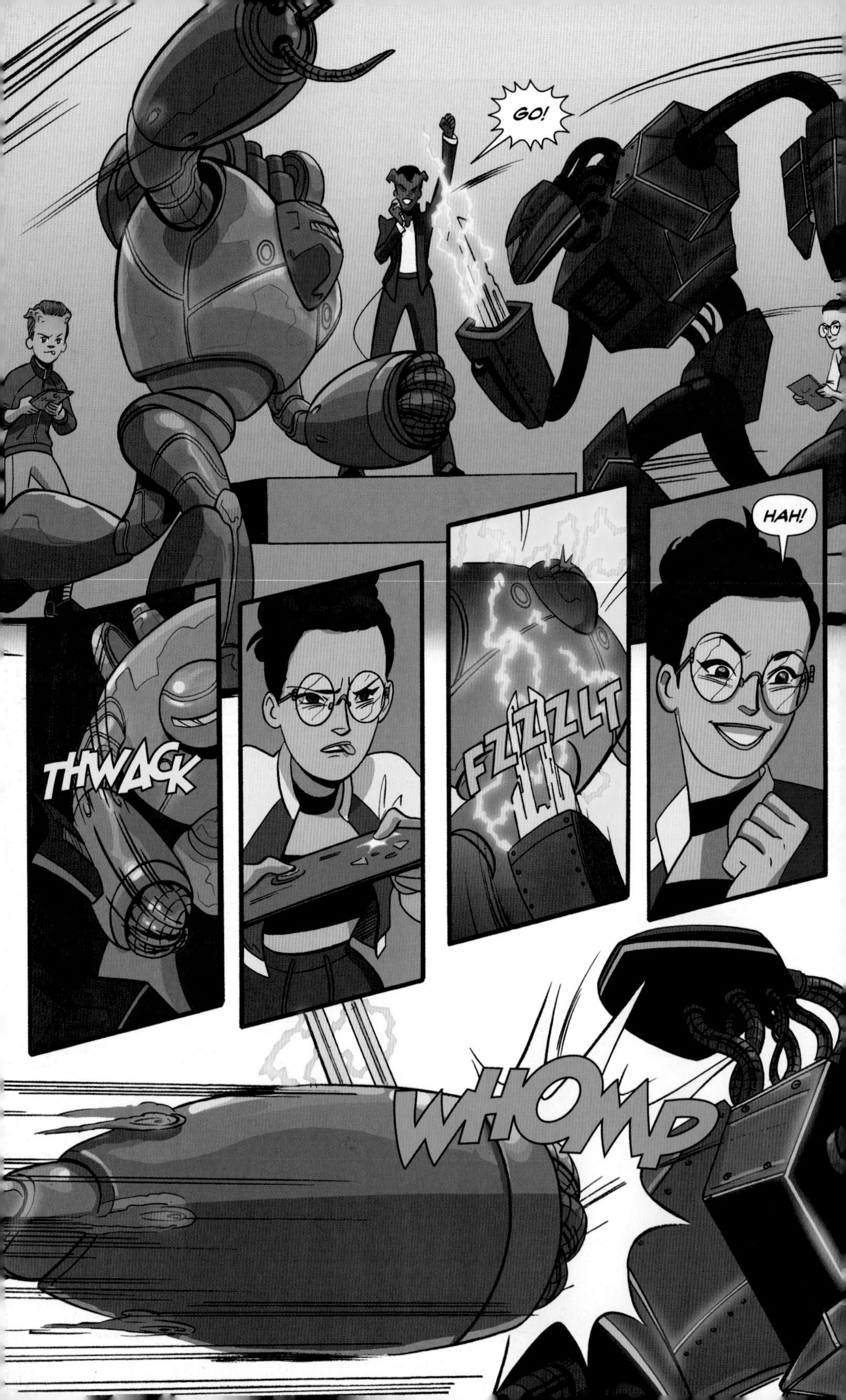
GO!
THWACK
FZZZZLT
HAH!
WHOMP

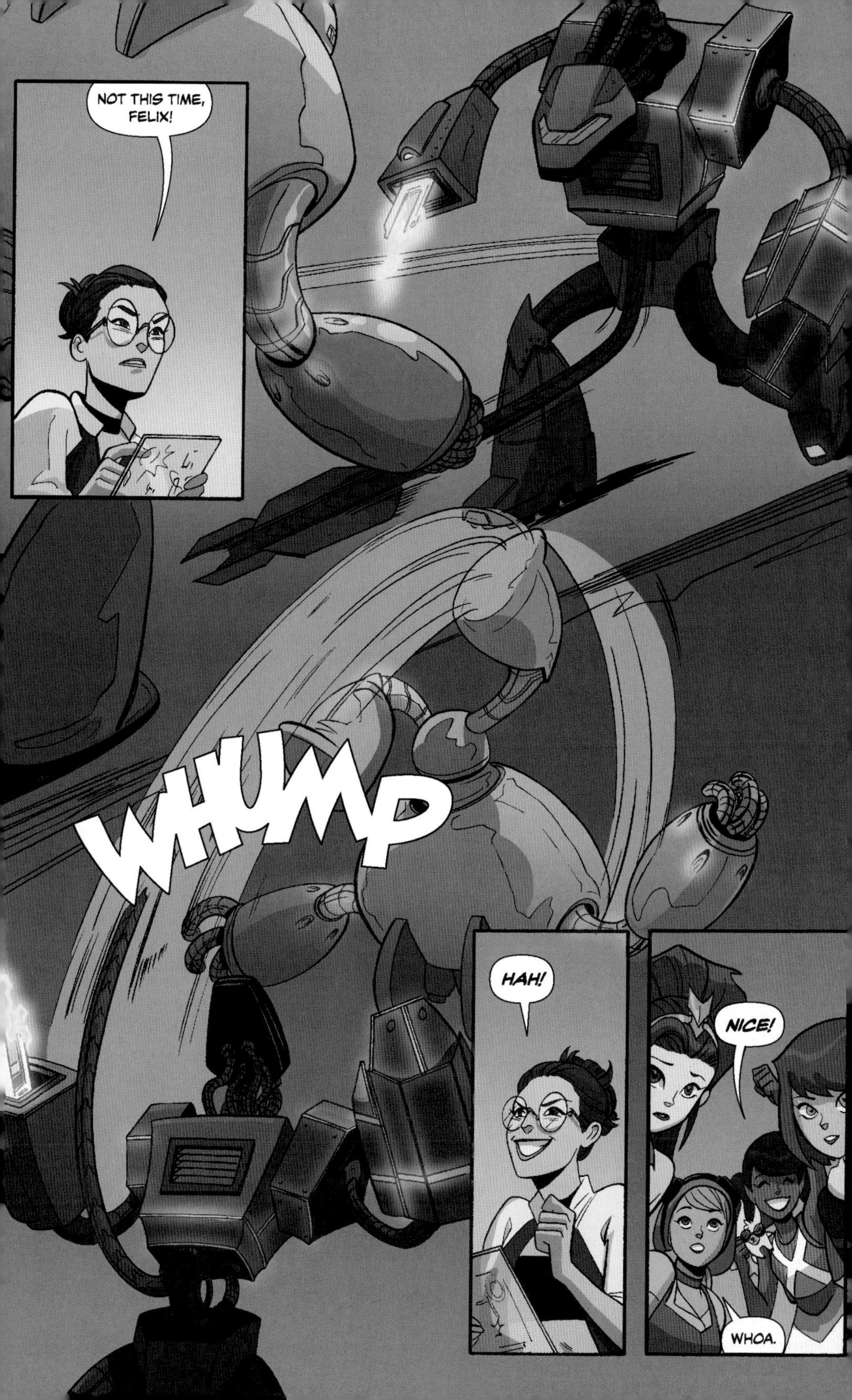
NOT THIS TIME, FELIX!
WHUMP
HAH!
NICE!
WHOA.

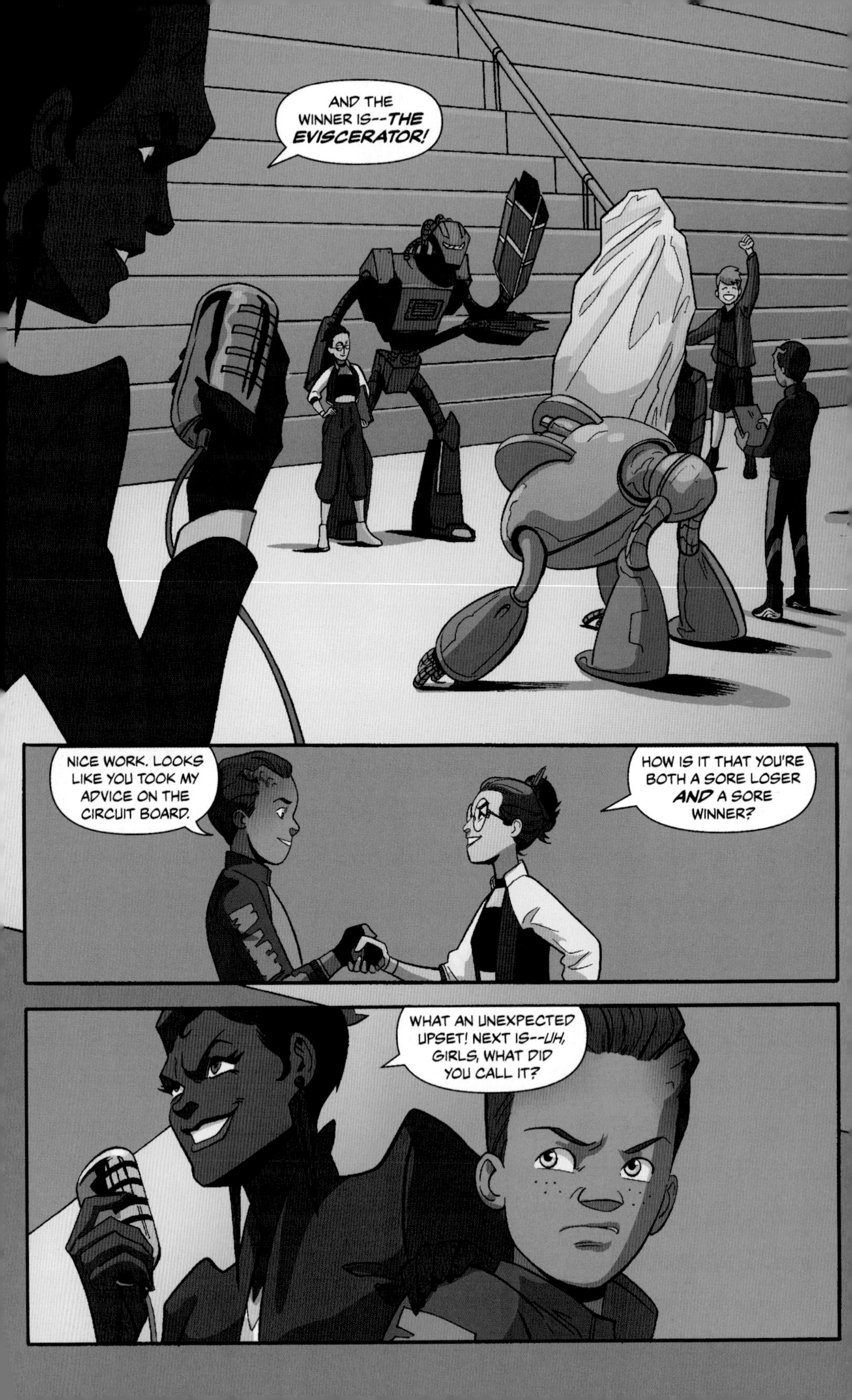
AND THE WINNER IS--THE EVISCERATOR!
NICE WORK. LOOKS LIKE YOU TOOK MY ADVICE ON THE CIRCUIT BOARD.
HOW IS IT THAT YOU'RE BOTH A SORE LOSER AND A SORE WINNER?
WHAT AN UNEXPECTED UPSET! NEXT IS--UH, GIRLS, WHAT DID YOU CALL IT?

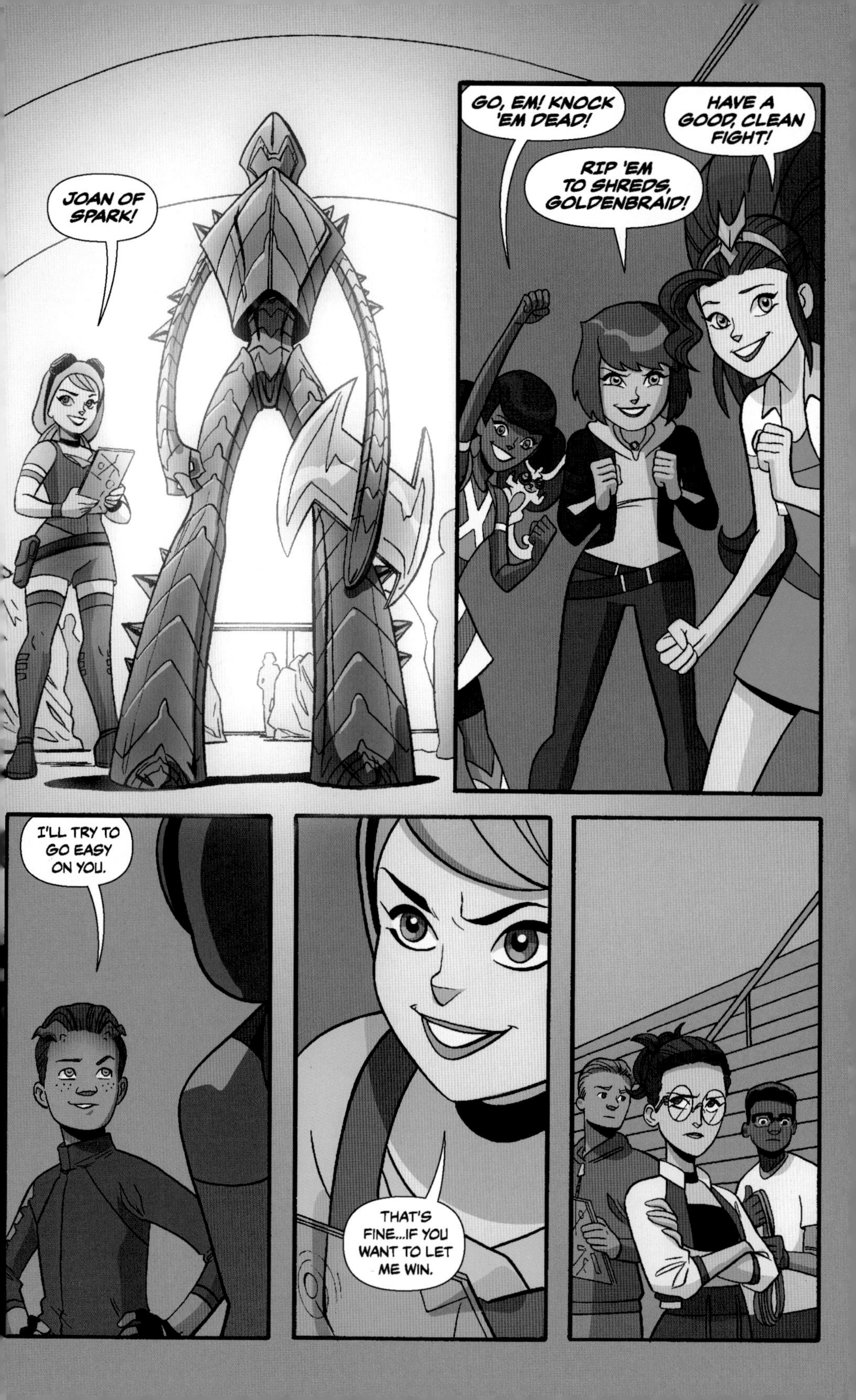
JOAN OF SPARK!
GO, EM! KNOCK 'EM DEAD!
HAVE A GOOD, CLEAN FIGHT!
RIP 'EM TO SHREDS, GOLDENBRAID!
I'LL TRY TO GO EASY ON YOU.
THAT'S FINE...IF YOU WANT TO LET ME WIN.

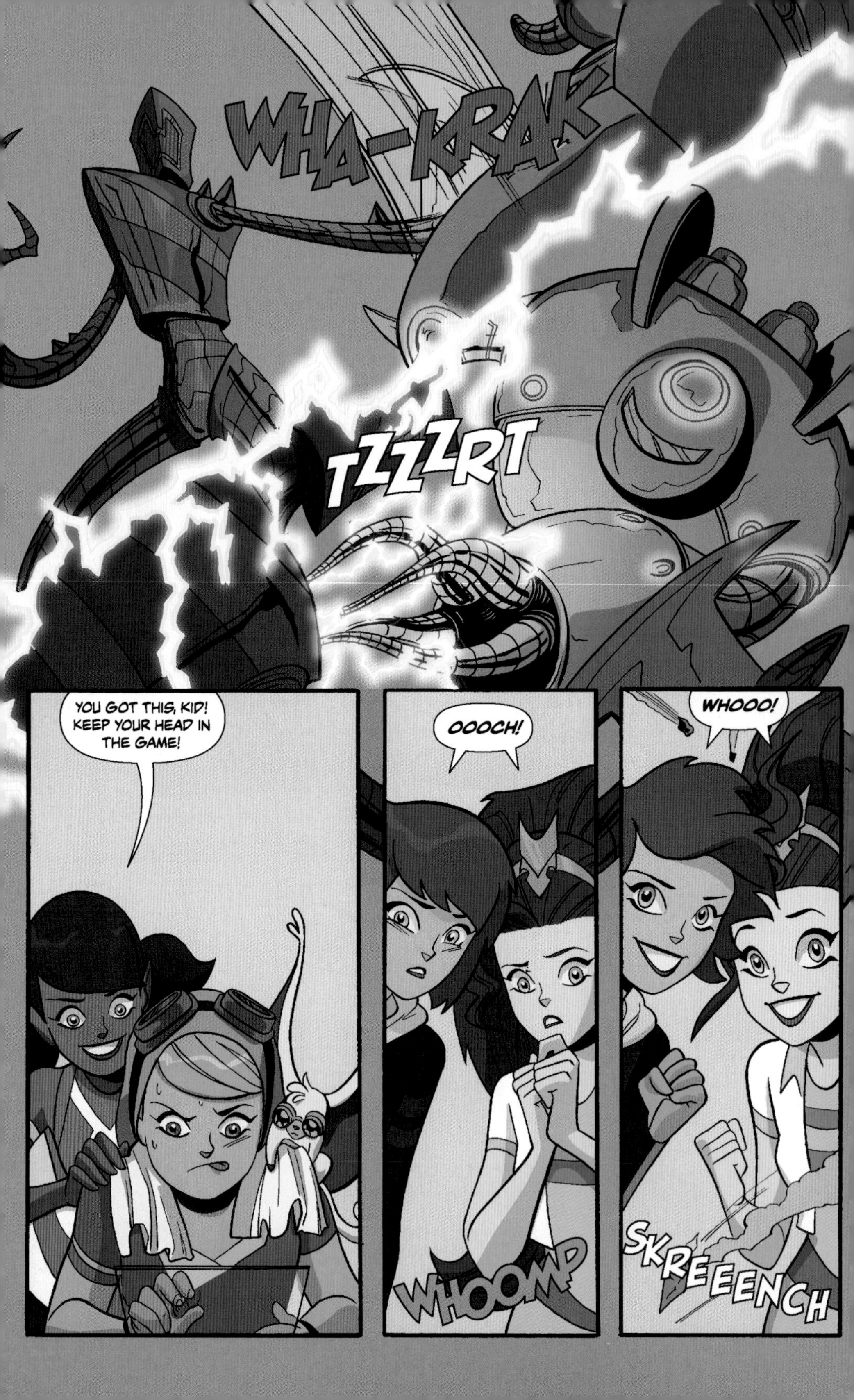
WHA-KRAK
TZZZRT
YOU GOT THIS, KID! KEEP YOUR HEAD IN THE GAME!
OOOCH!
WHOOMP
WHOOO!
SKREEEENCH

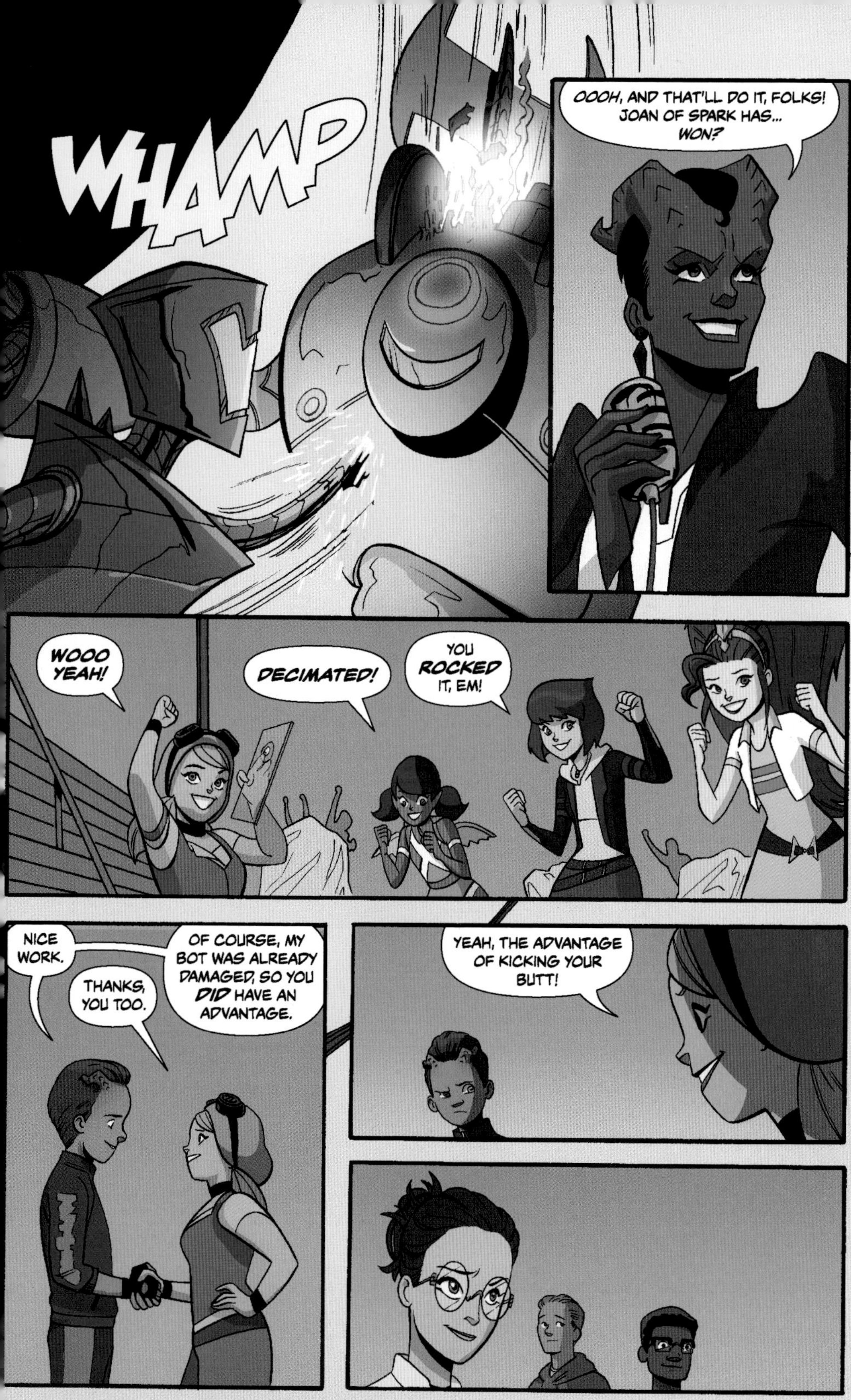
WHAMP
OOOH, AND THAT'LL DO IT, FOLKS! JOAN OF SPARK HAS... WON?
WOOO YEAH!
DECIMATED!
YOU ROCKED IT, EM!
NICE WORK.
THANKS, YOU TOO.
OF COURSE, MY BOT WAS ALREADY DAMAGED, SO YOU DID HAVE AN ADVANTAGE.
YEAH, THE ADVANTAGE OF KICKING YOUR BUTT!

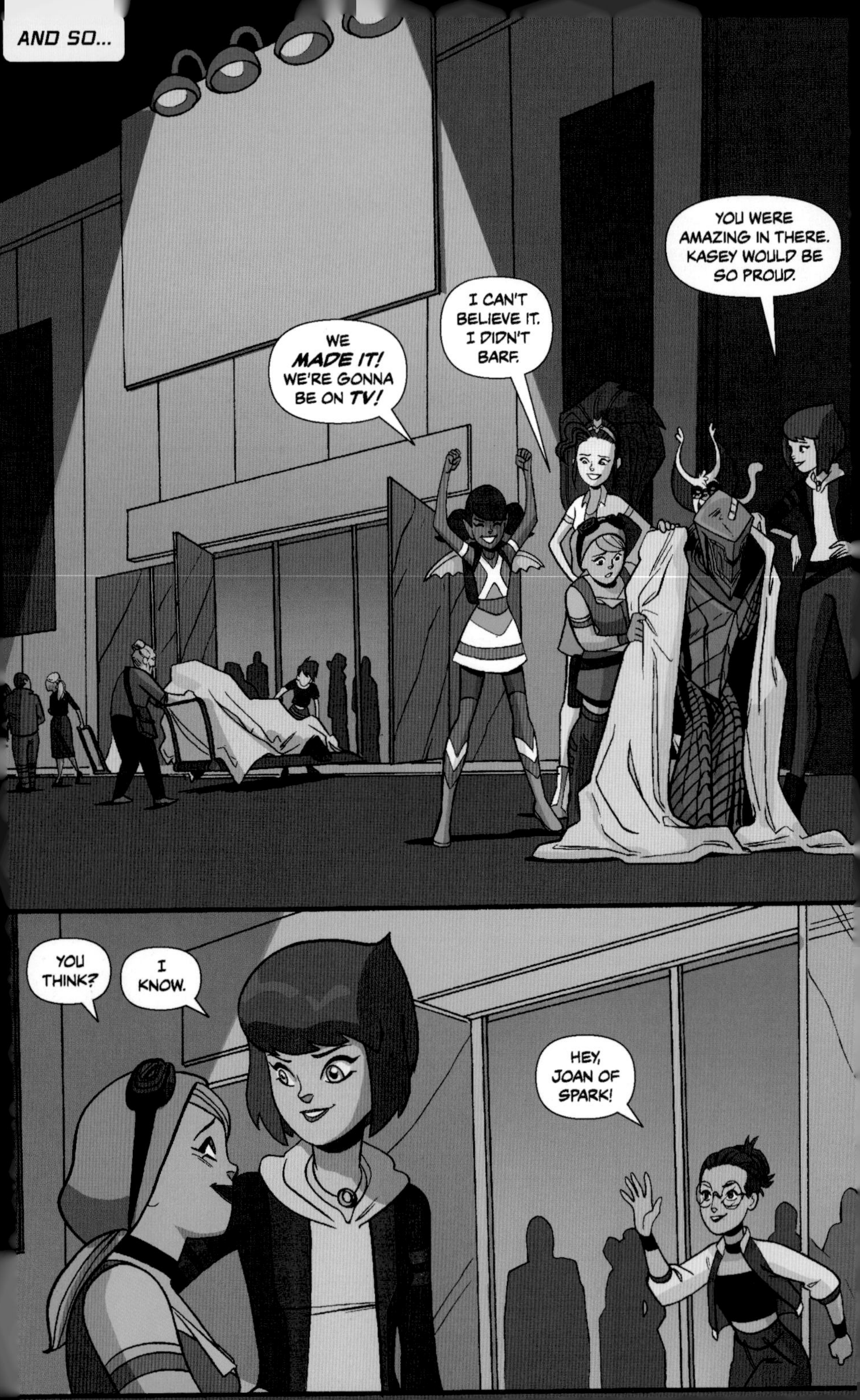
AND SO...
WE MADE IT! WE'RE GONNA BE ON TV!
I CAN'T BELIEVE IT. I DIDN'T BARF.
YOU WERE AMAZING IN THERE. KASEY WOULD BE SO PROUD.
YOU THINK?
I KNOW.
HEY, JOAN OF SPARK!

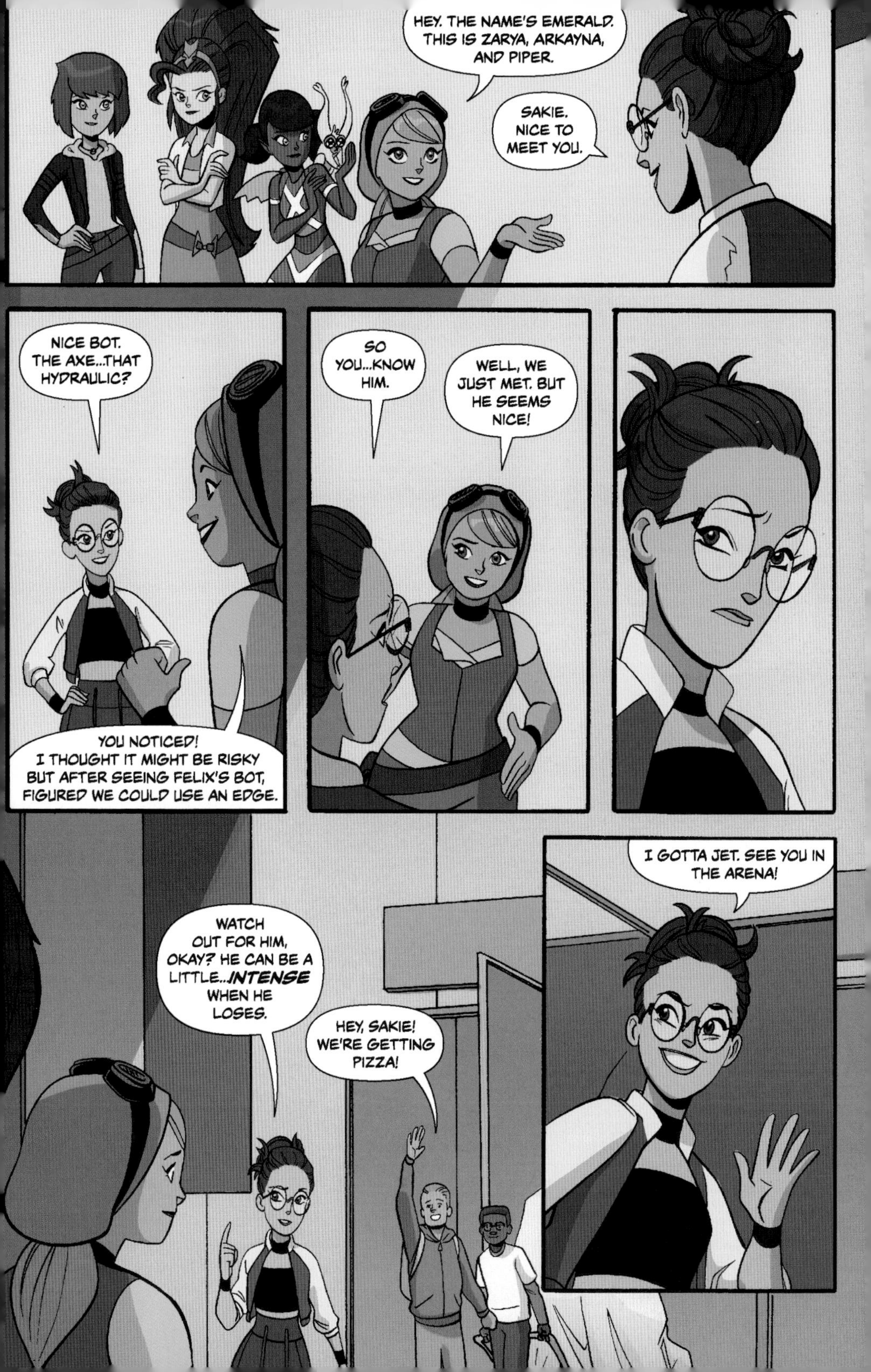
HEY. THE NAME'S EMERALD. THIS IS ZARYA, ARKAYNA, AND PIPER.
SAKIE. NICE TO MEET YOU.
NICE BOT. THE AXE...THAT HYDRAULIC?
YOU NOTICED! I THOUGHT IT MIGHT BE RISKY BUT AFTER SEEING FELIX'S BOT, FIGURED WE COULD USE AN EDGE.
SO YOU...KNOW HIM.
WELL, WE JUST MET. BUT HE SEEMS NICE!
WATCH OUT FOR HIM, OKAY? HE CAN BE A LITTLE...*INTENSE* WHEN HE LOSES.
HEY, SAKIE! WE'RE GETTING PIZZA!
I GOTTA JET. SEE YOU IN THE ARENA!

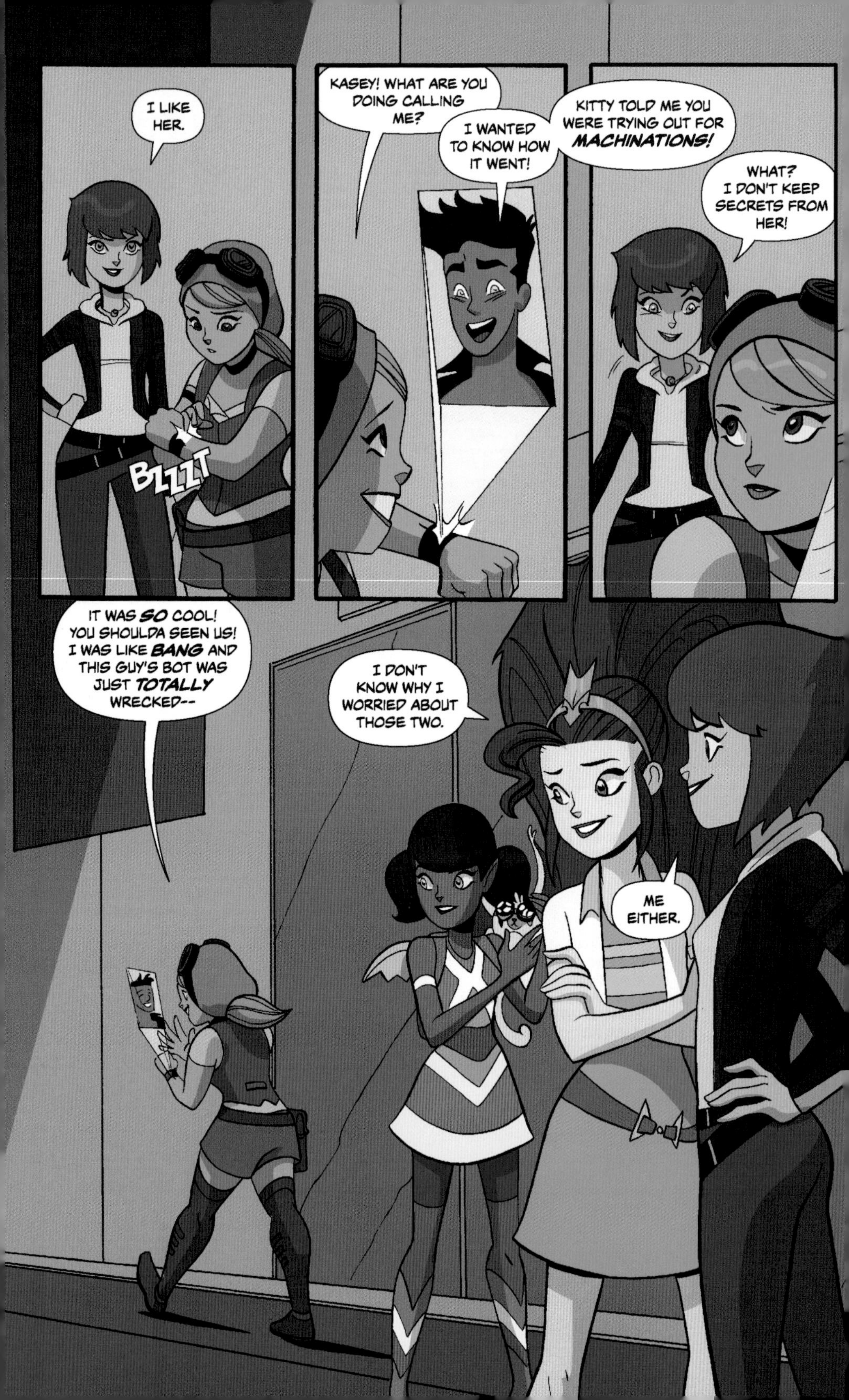
I LIKE HER.
BZZZT
KASEY! WHAT ARE YOU DOING CALLING ME?
I WANTED TO KNOW HOW IT WENT!
KITTY TOLD ME YOU WERE TRYING OUT FOR *MACHINATIONS!*
WHAT? I DON'T KEEP SECRETS FROM HER!
IT WAS *SO* COOL! YOU SHOULDA SEEN US! I WAS LIKE *BANG* AND THIS GUY'S BOT WAS JUST *TOTALLY* WRECKED--
I DON'T KNOW WHY I WORRIED ABOUT THOSE TWO.
ME EITHER.

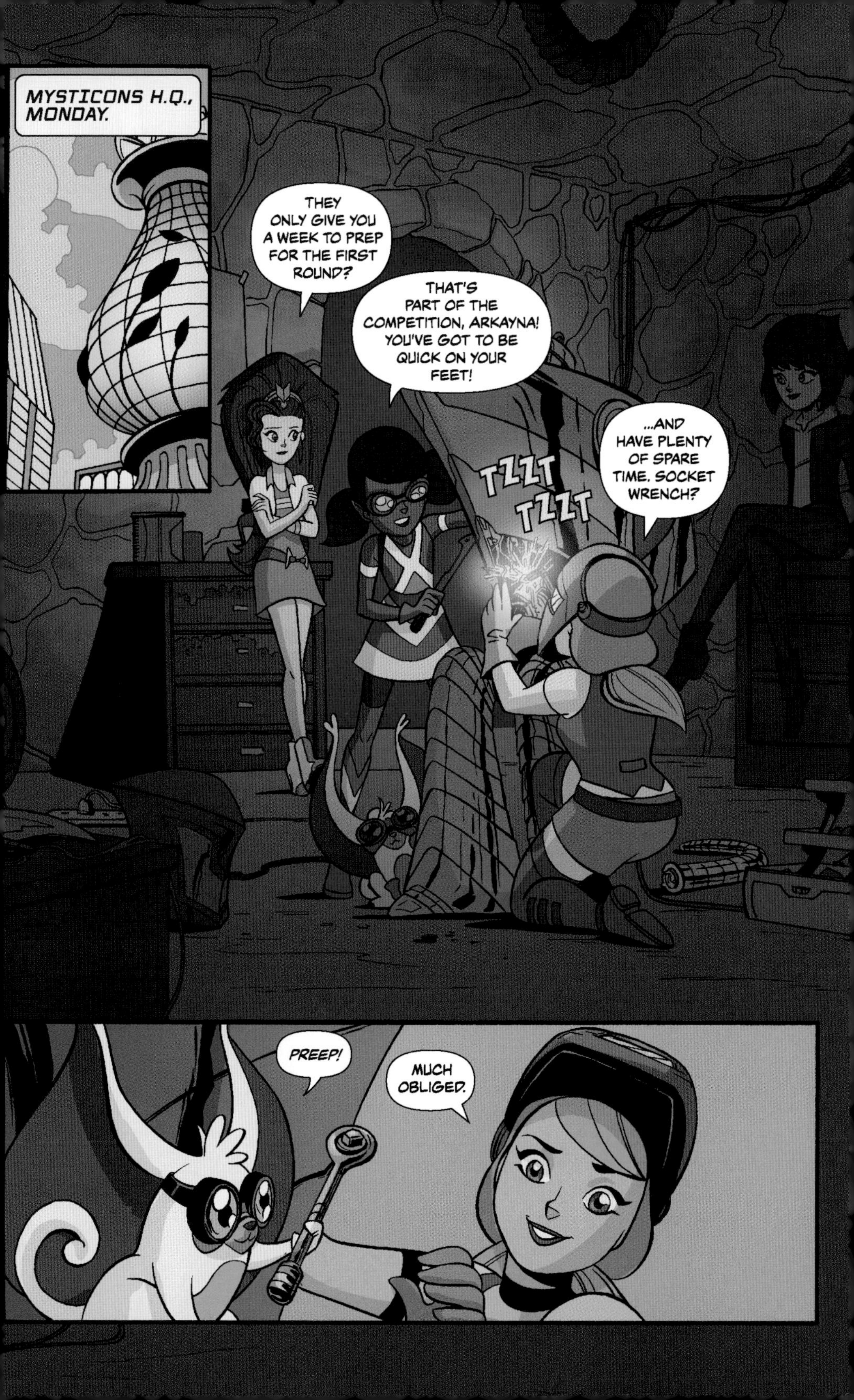
MYSTICONS H.Q., MONDAY.
THEY ONLY GIVE YOU A WEEK TO PREP FOR THE FIRST ROUND?
THAT'S PART OF THE COMPETITION, ARKAYNA! YOU'VE GOT TO BE QUICK ON YOUR FEET!
TZZT TZZT
...AND HAVE PLENTY OF SPARE TIME. SOCKET WRENCH?
PREEP!
MUCH OBLIGED.

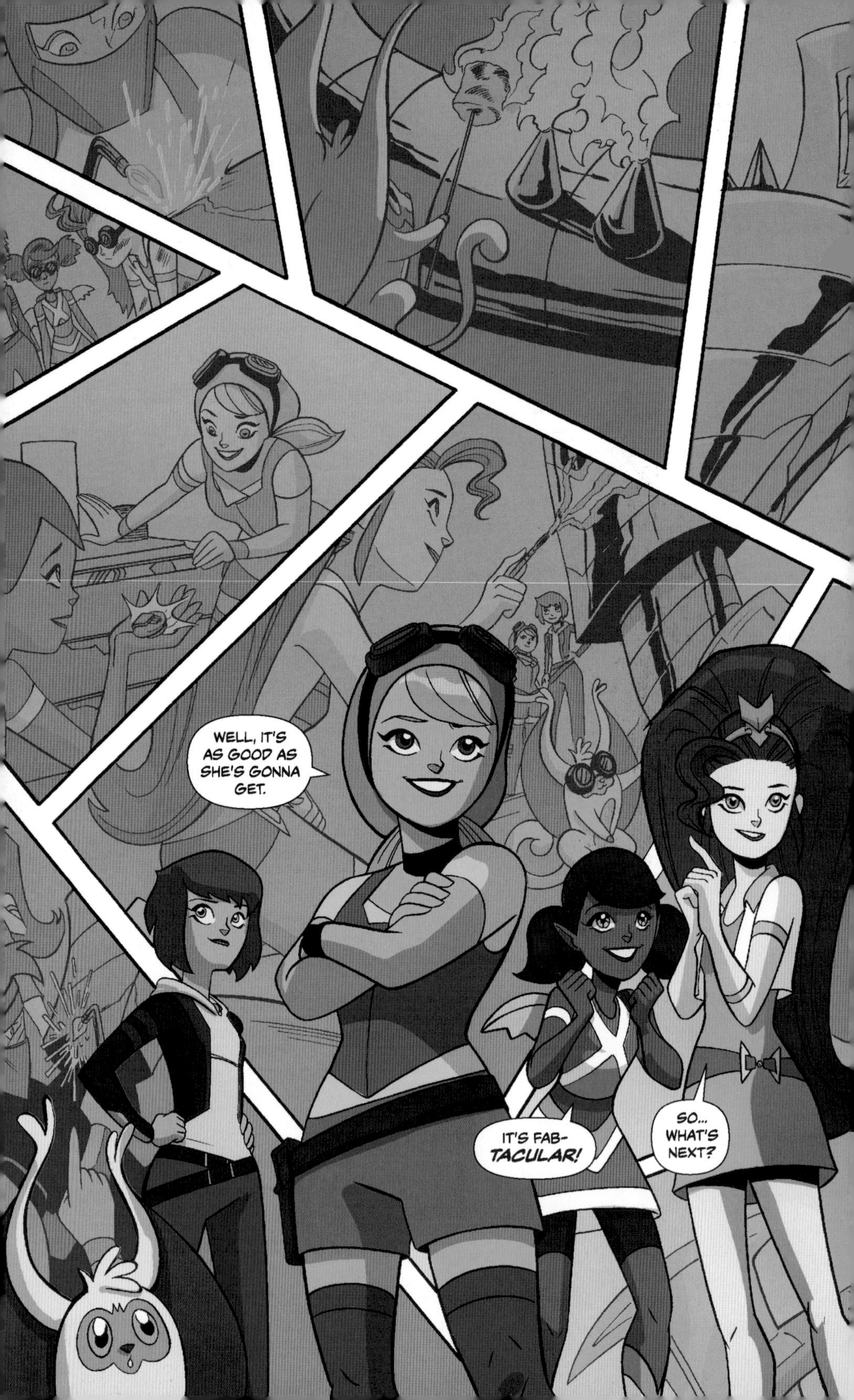

WELL, IT'S AS GOOD AS SHE'S GONNA GET.
IT'S FAB-*TACULAR!*
SO... WHAT'S NEXT?

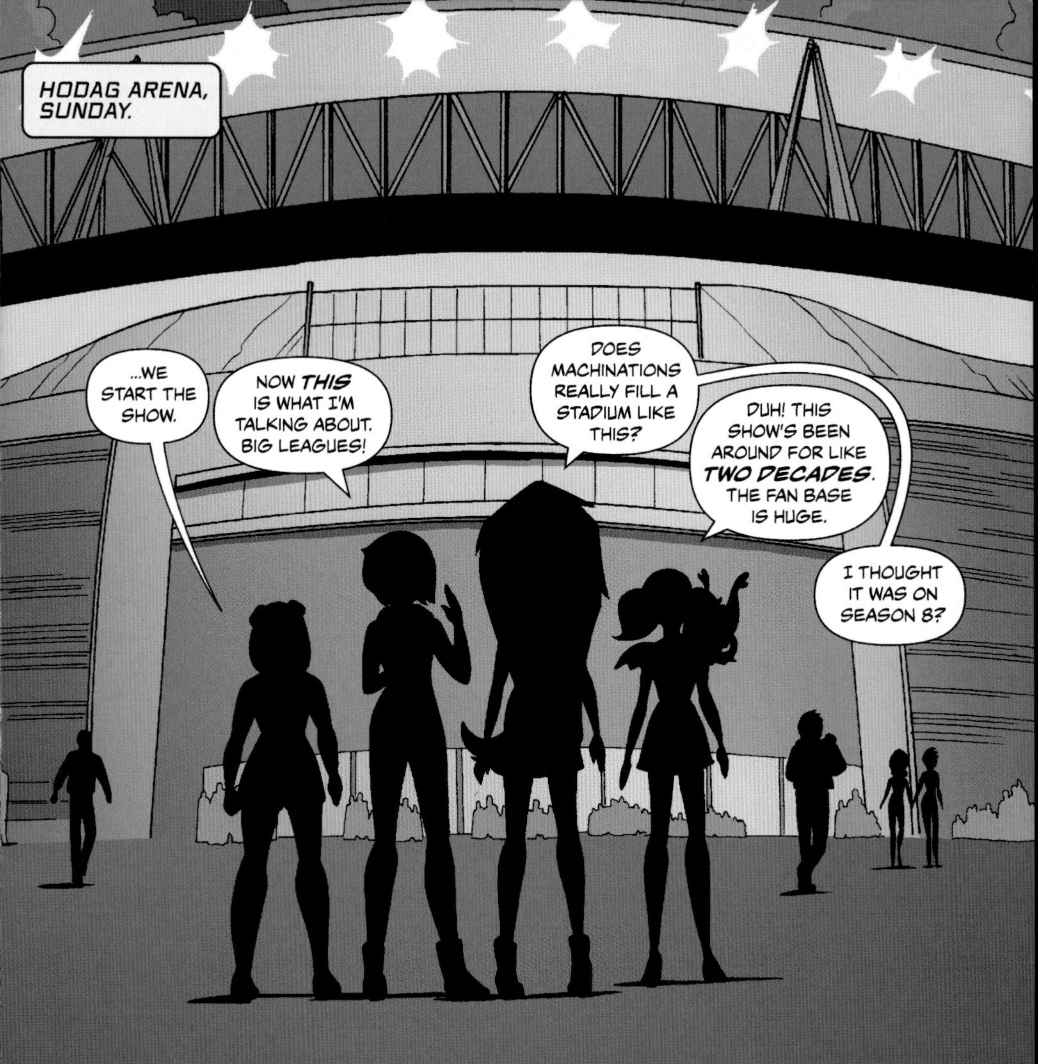
HODAG ARENA, SUNDAY.
...WE START THE SHOW.
NOW THIS IS WHAT I'M TALKING ABOUT. BIG LEAGUES!
DOES MACHINATIONS REALLY FILL A STADIUM LIKE THIS?
DUH! THIS SHOW'S BEEN AROUND FOR LIKE TWO DECADES. THE FAN BASE IS HUGE.
I THOUGHT IT WAS ON SEASON 8?
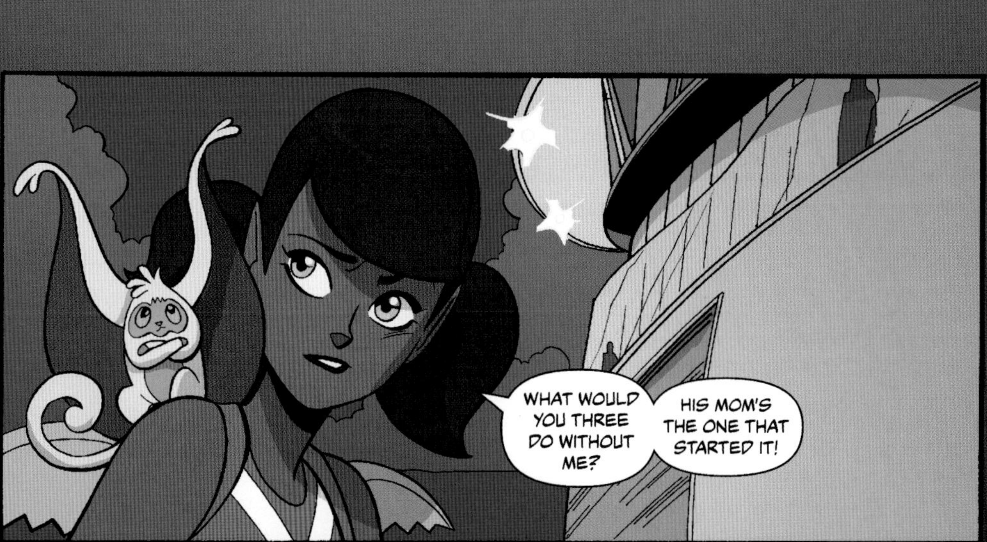
WHAT WOULD YOU THREE DO WITHOUT ME?
HIS MOM'S THE ONE THAT STARTED IT!

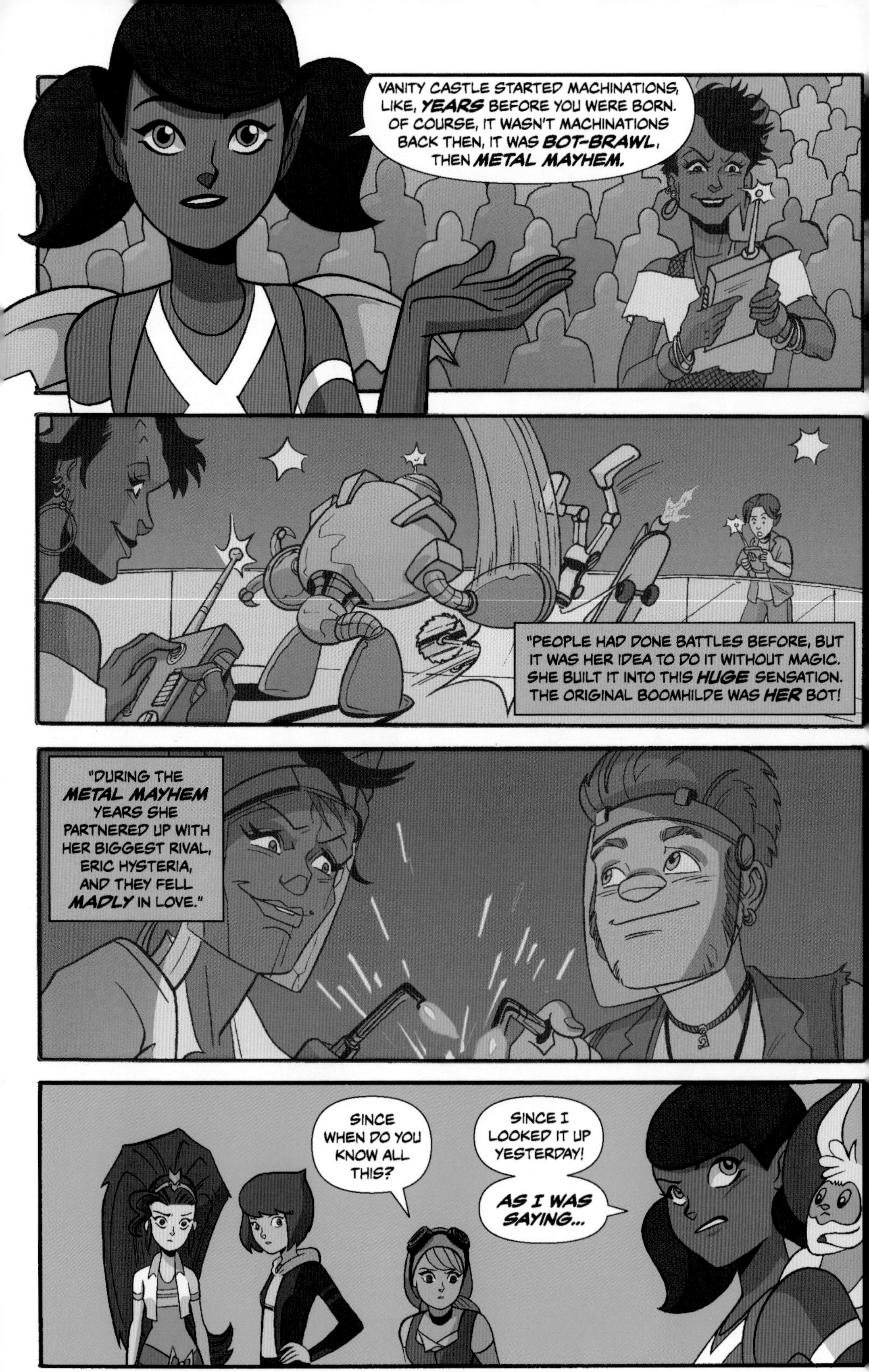
VANITY CASTLE STARTED MACHINATIONS, LIKE, YEARS BEFORE YOU WERE BORN. OF COURSE, IT WASN'T MACHINATIONS BACK THEN, IT WAS BOT-BRAWL, THEN METAL MAYHEM.
"PEOPLE HAD DONE BATTLES BEFORE, BUT IT WAS HER IDEA TO DO IT WITHOUT MAGIC. SHE BUILT IT INTO THIS HUGE SENSATION. THE ORIGINAL BOOMHILDE WAS HER BOT!
"DURING THE METAL MAYHEM YEARS SHE PARTNERED UP WITH HER BIGGEST RIVAL, ERIC HYSTERIA, AND THEY FELL MADLY IN LOVE."
SINCE WHEN DO YOU KNOW ALL THIS?
SINCE I LOOKED IT UP YESTERDAY!
AS I WAS SAYING...

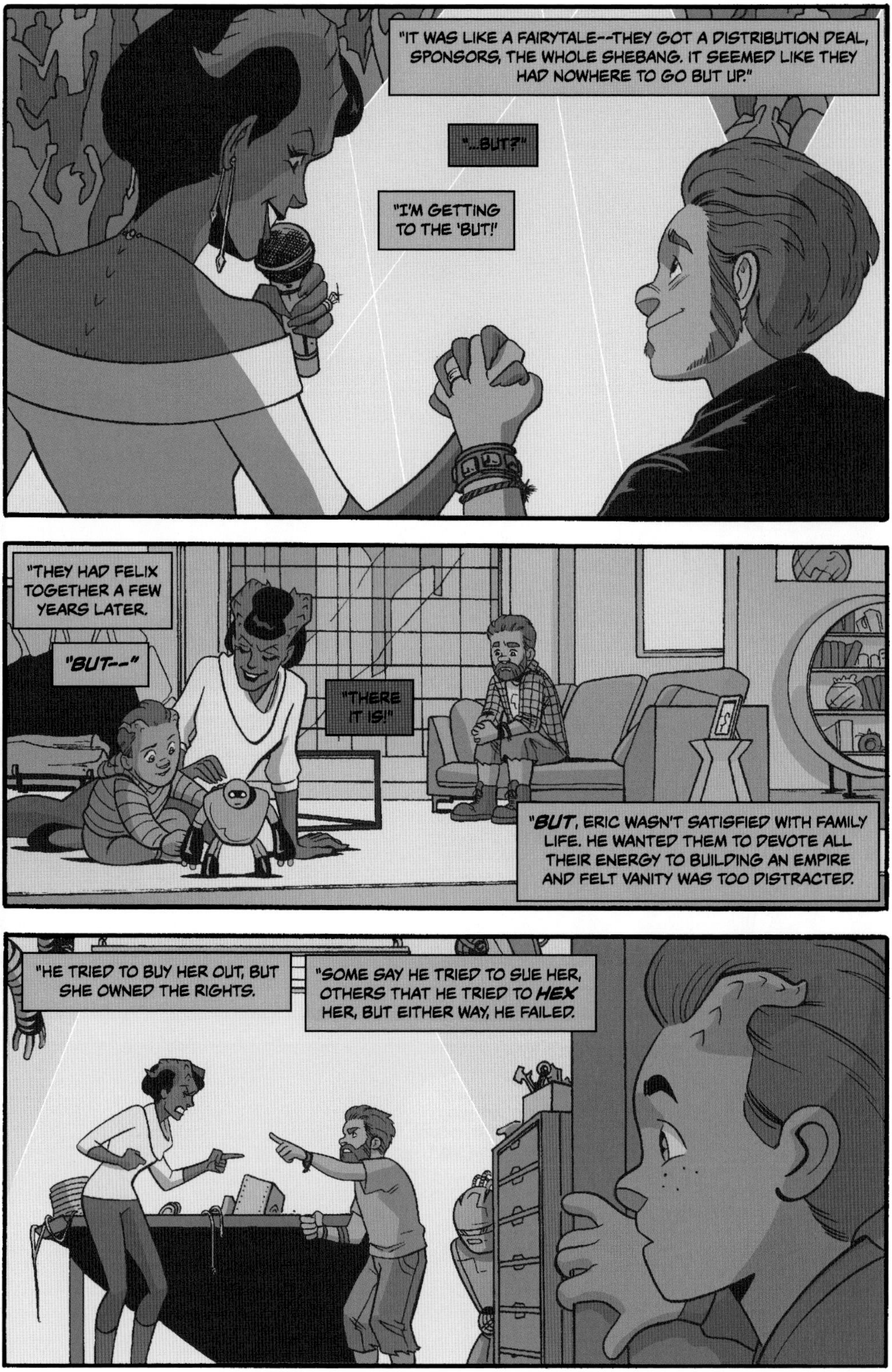
"IT WAS LIKE A FAIRYTALE--THEY GOT A DISTRIBUTION DEAL, SPONSORS, THE WHOLE SHEBANG. IT SEEMED LIKE THEY HAD NOWHERE TO GO BUT UP."
"...BUT?"
"I'M GETTING TO THE 'BUT!'
"THEY HAD FELIX TOGETHER A FEW YEARS LATER.
"BUT--"
"THERE IT IS!"
"BUT, ERIC WASN'T SATISFIED WITH FAMILY LIFE. HE WANTED THEM TO DEVOTE ALL THEIR ENERGY TO BUILDING AN EMPIRE AND FELT VANITY WAS TOO DISTRACTED.
"HE TRIED TO BUY HER OUT, BUT SHE OWNED THE RIGHTS.
"SOME SAY HE TRIED TO SUE HER, OTHERS THAT HE TRIED TO HEX HER, BUT EITHER WAY, HE FAILED.

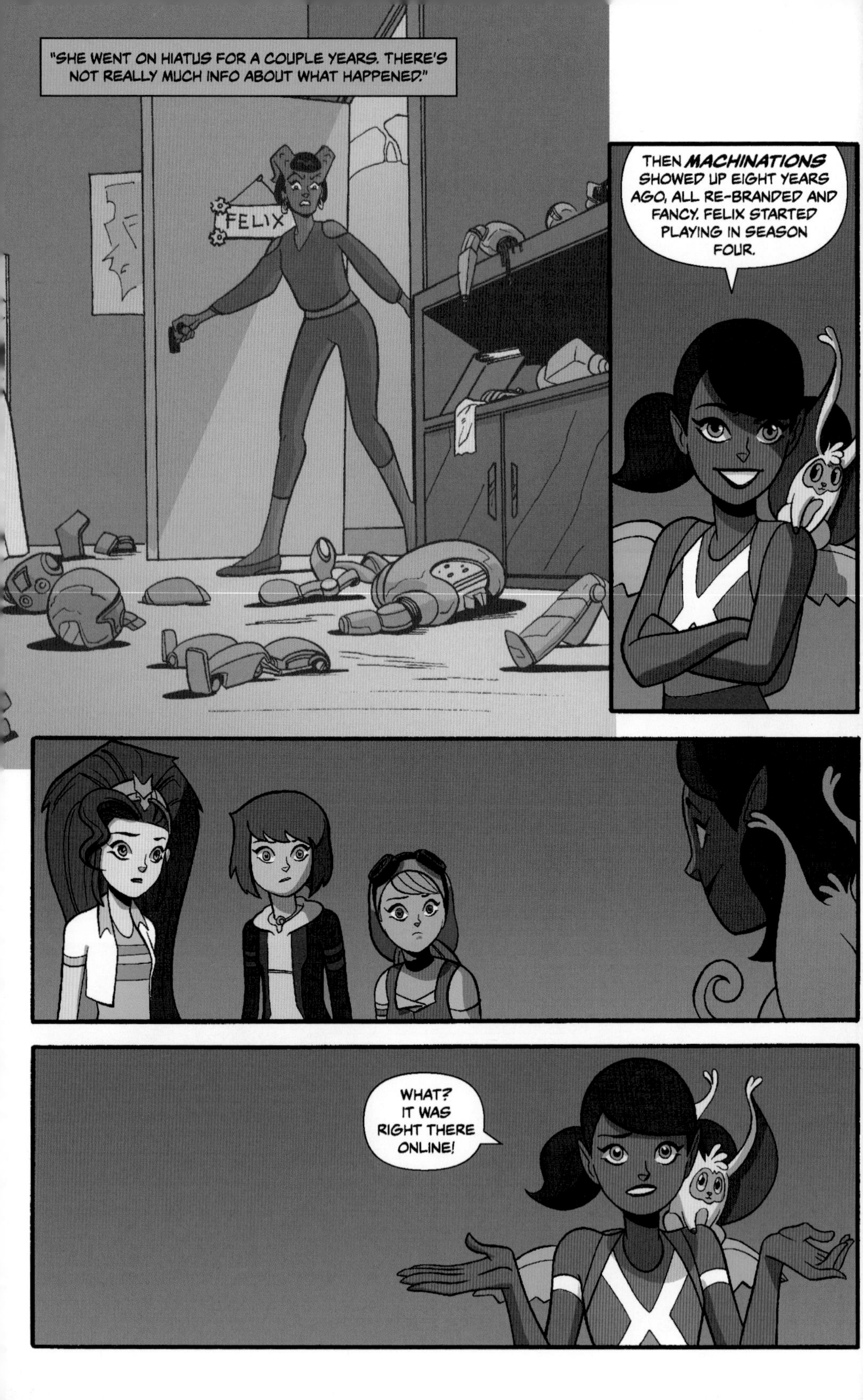
"SHE WENT ON HIATUS FOR A COUPLE YEARS. THERE'S NOT REALLY MUCH INFO ABOUT WHAT HAPPENED."
FELIX
THEN MACHINATIONS SHOWED UP EIGHT YEARS AGO, ALL RE-BRANDED AND FANCY. FELIX STARTED PLAYING IN SEASON FOUR.
WHAT? IT WAS RIGHT THERE ONLINE!

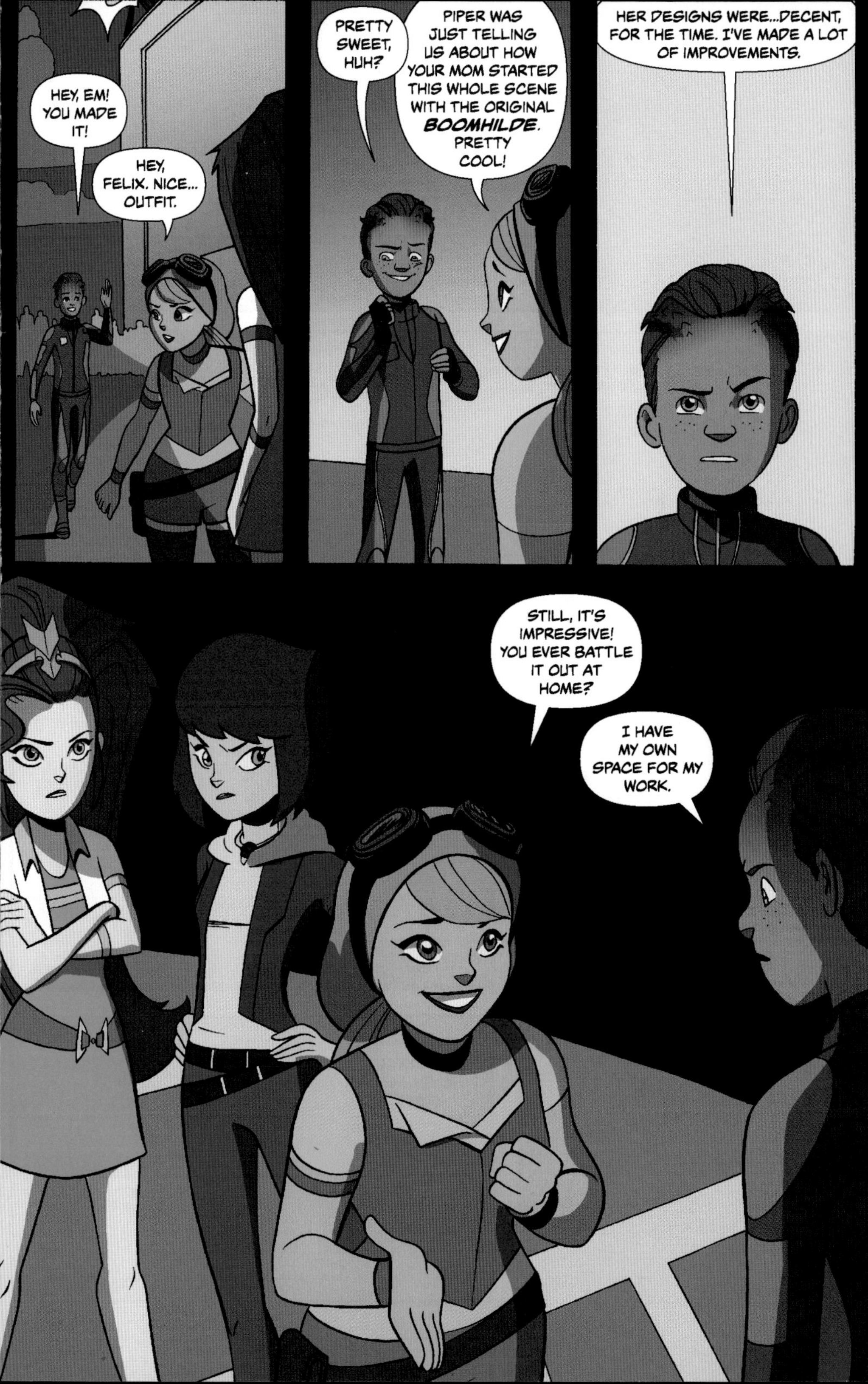
HEY, EM! YOU MADE IT!
HEY, FELIX. NICE... OUTFIT.
PRETTY SWEET, HUH?
PIPER WAS JUST TELLING US ABOUT HOW YOUR MOM STARTED THIS WHOLE SCENE WITH THE ORIGINAL **BOOMHILDE**. PRETTY COOL!
HER DESIGNS WERE...DECENT, FOR THE TIME. I'VE MADE A LOT OF IMPROVEMENTS.
STILL, IT'S IMPRESSIVE! YOU EVER BATTLE IT OUT AT HOME?
I HAVE MY OWN SPACE FOR MY WORK.

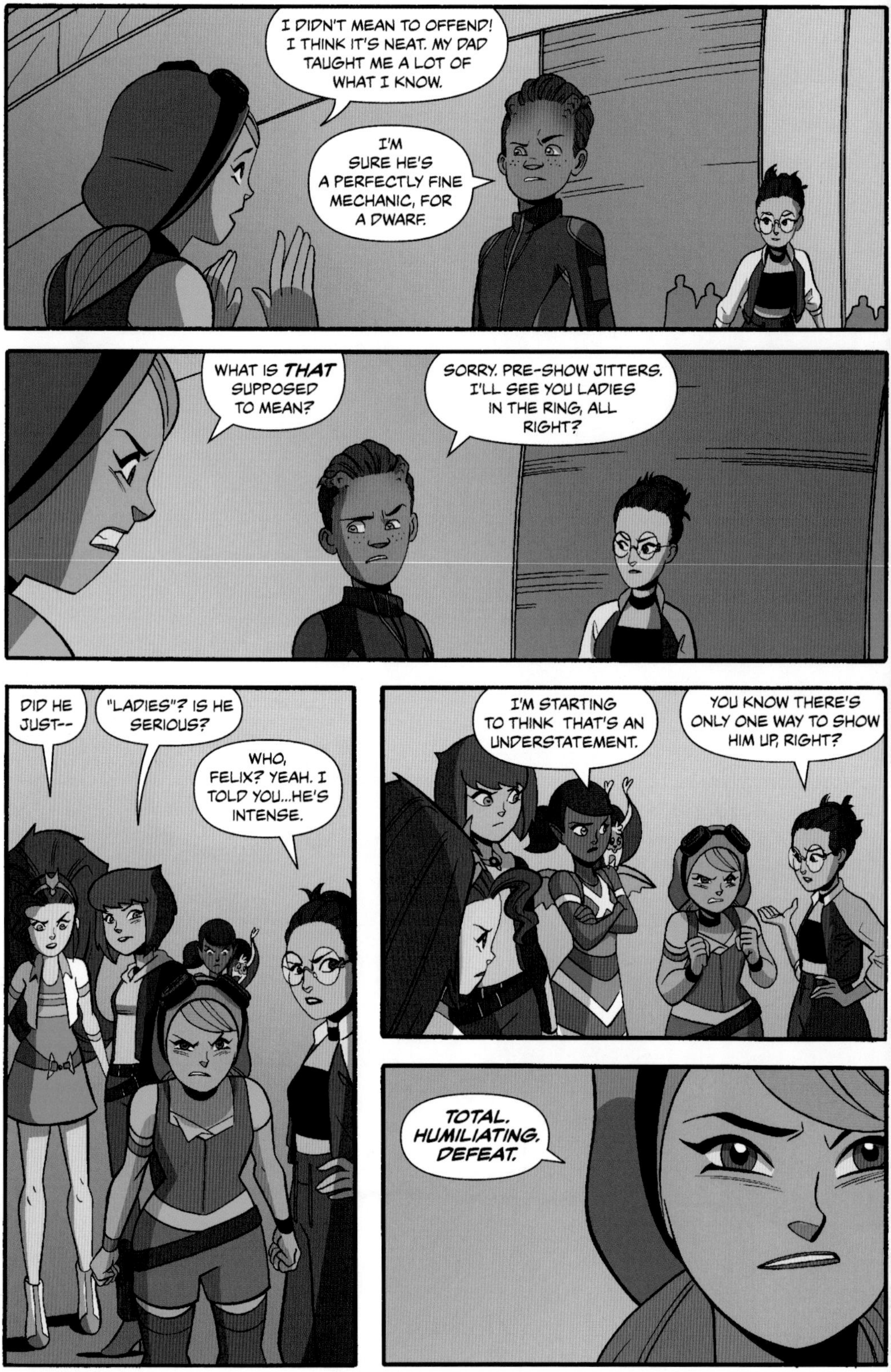

I DIDN'T MEAN TO OFFEND! I THINK IT'S NEAT. MY DAD TAUGHT ME A LOT OF WHAT I KNOW.
I'M SURE HE'S A PERFECTLY FINE MECHANIC, FOR A DWARF.
WHAT IS *THAT* SUPPOSED TO MEAN?
SORRY. PRE-SHOW JITTERS. I'LL SEE YOU LADIES IN THE RING, ALL RIGHT?
DID HE JUST--
"LADIES"? IS HE SERIOUS?
WHO, FELIX? YEAH. I TOLD YOU...HE'S INTENSE.
I'M STARTING TO THINK THAT'S AN UNDERSTATEMENT.
YOU KNOW THERE'S ONLY ONE WAY TO SHOW HIM UP, RIGHT?
TOTAL. HUMILIATING. DEFEAT.

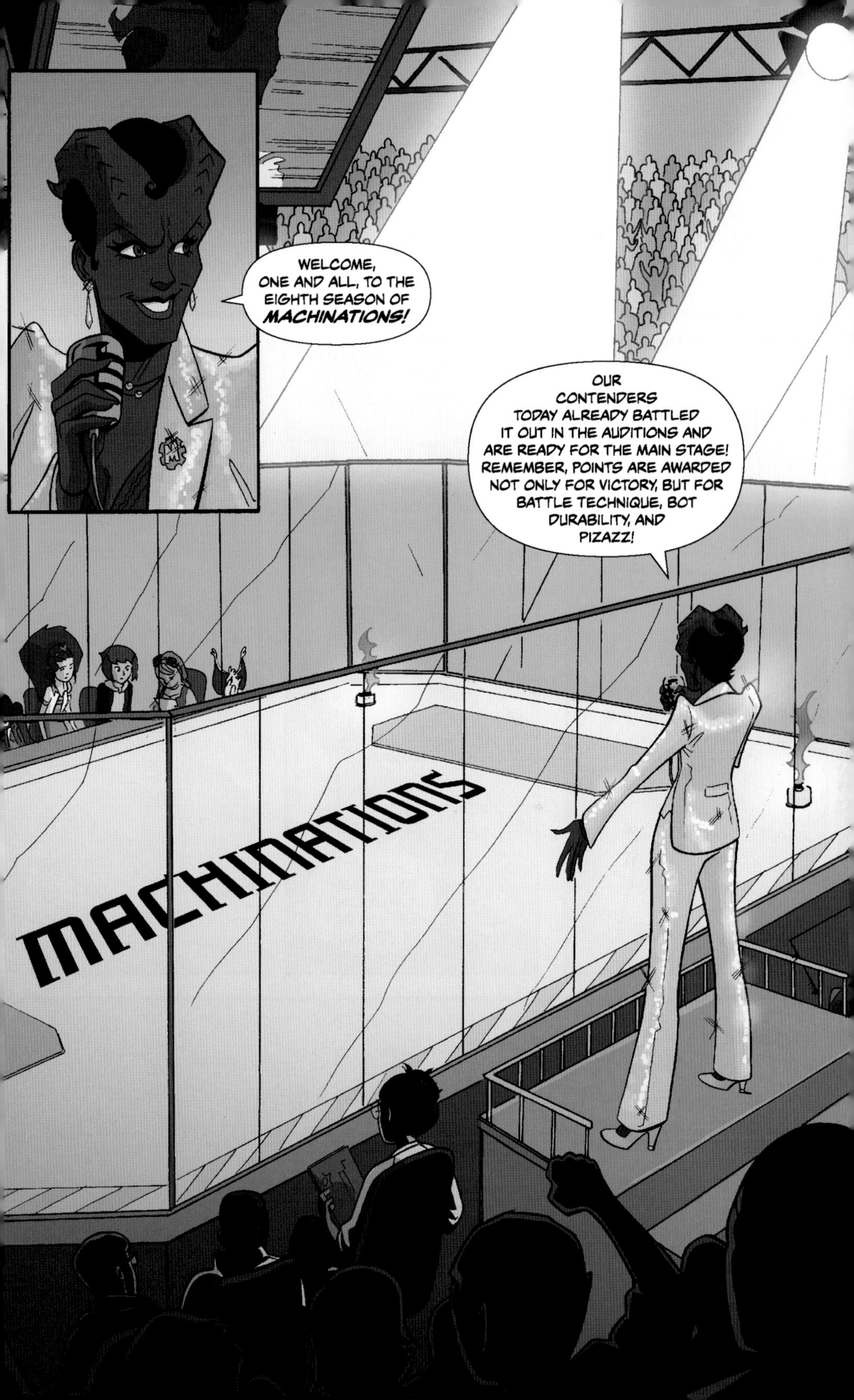
WELCOME, ONE AND ALL, TO THE EIGHTH SEASON OF MACHINATIONS!
OUR CONTENDERS TODAY ALREADY BATTLED IT OUT IN THE AUDITIONS AND ARE READY FOR THE MAIN STAGE! REMEMBER, POINTS ARE AWARDED NOT ONLY FOR VICTORY, BUT FOR BATTLE TECHNIQUE, BOT DURABILITY, AND PIZAZZ!
MACHINATIONS

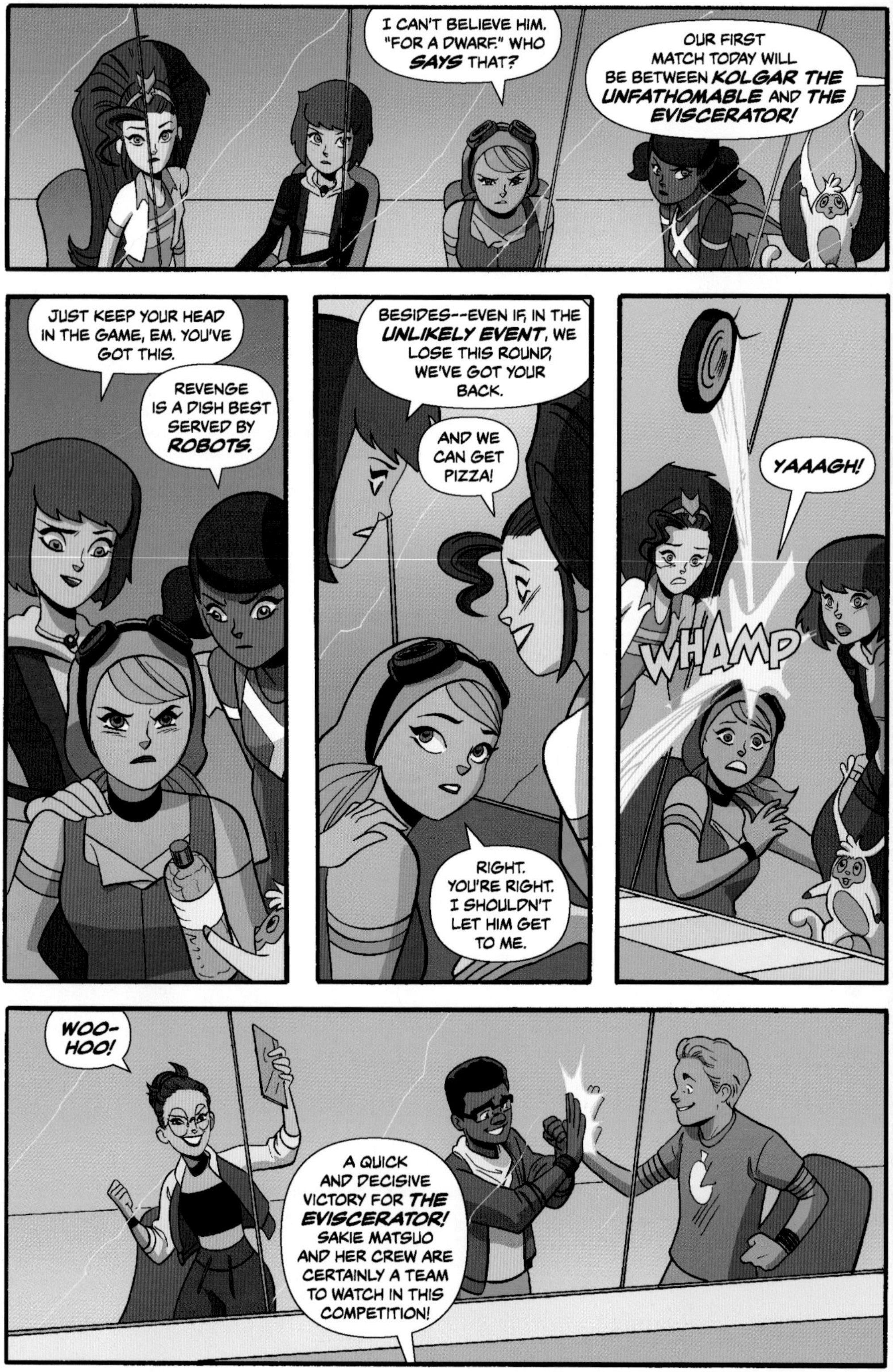

I CAN'T BELIEVE HIM. "FOR A DWARF." WHO SAYS THAT?
OUR FIRST MATCH TODAY WILL BE BETWEEN KOLGAR THE UNFATHOMABLE AND THE EVISCERATOR!
JUST KEEP YOUR HEAD IN THE GAME, EM. YOU'VE GOT THIS.
REVENGE IS A DISH BEST SERVED BY ROBOTS.
BESIDES--EVEN IF, IN THE UNLIKELY EVENT, WE LOSE THIS ROUND, WE'VE GOT YOUR BACK.
AND WE CAN GET PIZZA!
RIGHT. YOU'RE RIGHT. I SHOULDN'T LET HIM GET TO ME.
YAAAGH!
WHAMP
WOO-HOO!
A QUICK AND DECISIVE VICTORY FOR THE EVISCERATOR! SAKIE MATSUO AND HER CREW ARE CERTAINLY A TEAM TO WATCH IN THIS COMPETITION!

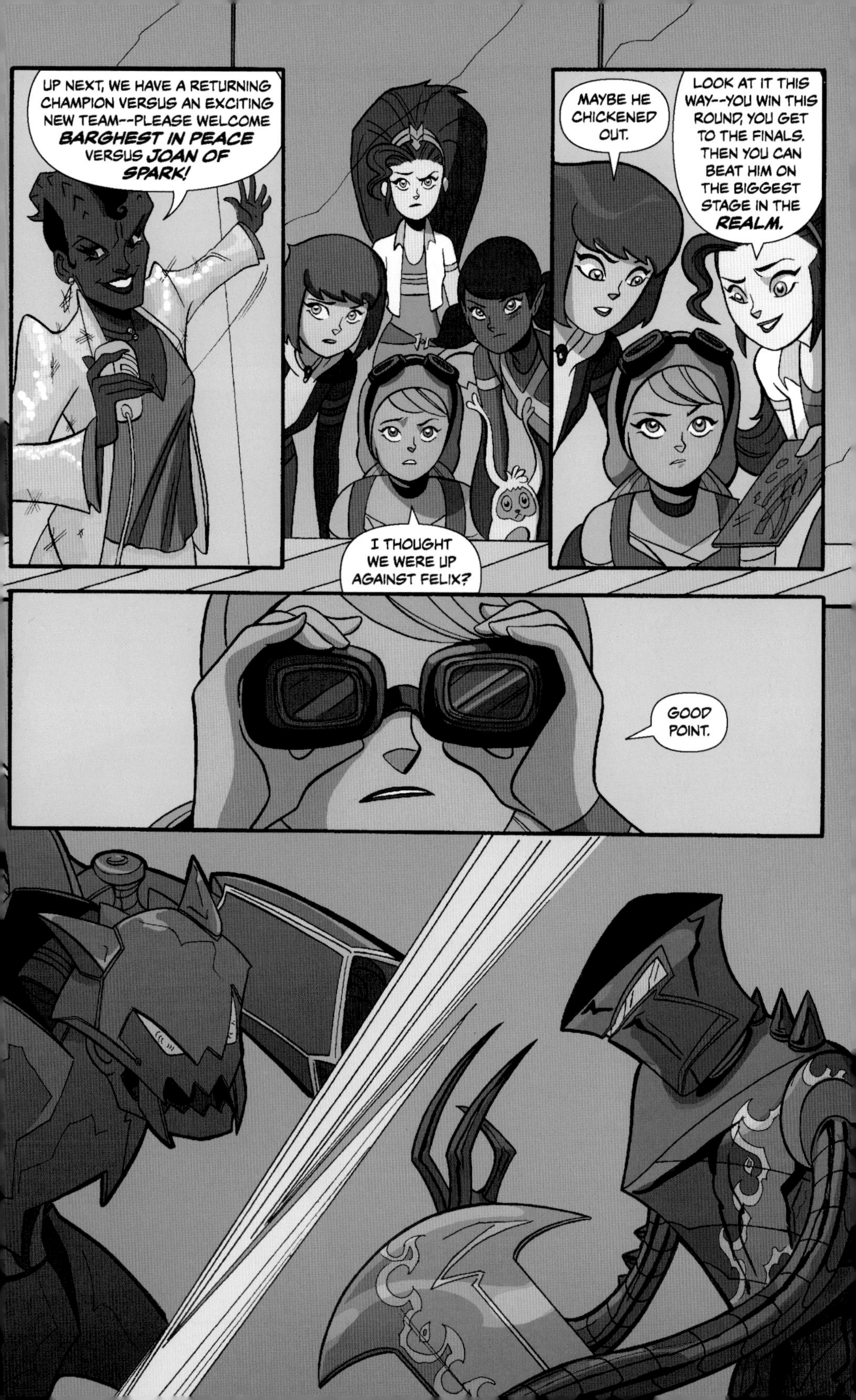
UP NEXT, WE HAVE A RETURNING CHAMPION VERSUS AN EXCITING NEW TEAM--PLEASE WELCOME **BARGHEST IN PEACE** VERSUS **JOAN OF SPARK!**
I THOUGHT WE WERE UP AGAINST FELIX?
MAYBE HE CHICKENED OUT.
LOOK AT IT THIS WAY--YOU WIN THIS ROUND, YOU GET TO THE FINALS. THEN YOU CAN BEAT HIM ON THE BIGGEST STAGE IN THE **REALM.**
GOOD POINT.

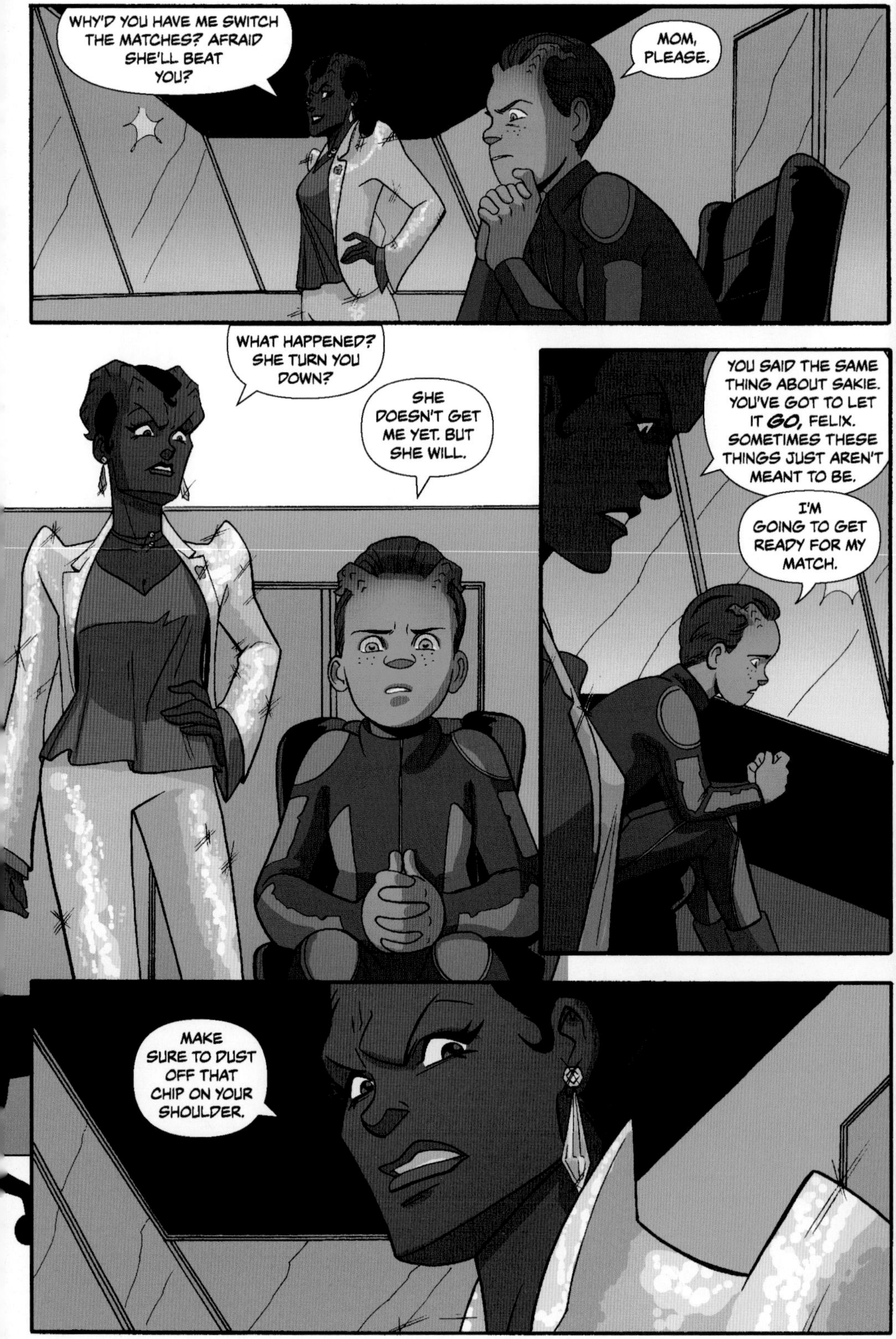
WHY'D YOU HAVE ME SWITCH THE MATCHES? AFRAID SHE'LL BEAT YOU?
MOM, PLEASE.
WHAT HAPPENED? SHE TURN YOU DOWN?
SHE DOESN'T GET ME YET. BUT SHE WILL.
YOU SAID THE SAME THING ABOUT SAKIE. YOU'VE GOT TO LET IT GO, FELIX. SOMETIMES THESE THINGS JUST AREN'T MEANT TO BE.
I'M GOING TO GET READY FOR MY MATCH.
MAKE SURE TO DUST OFF THAT CHIP ON YOUR SHOULDER.

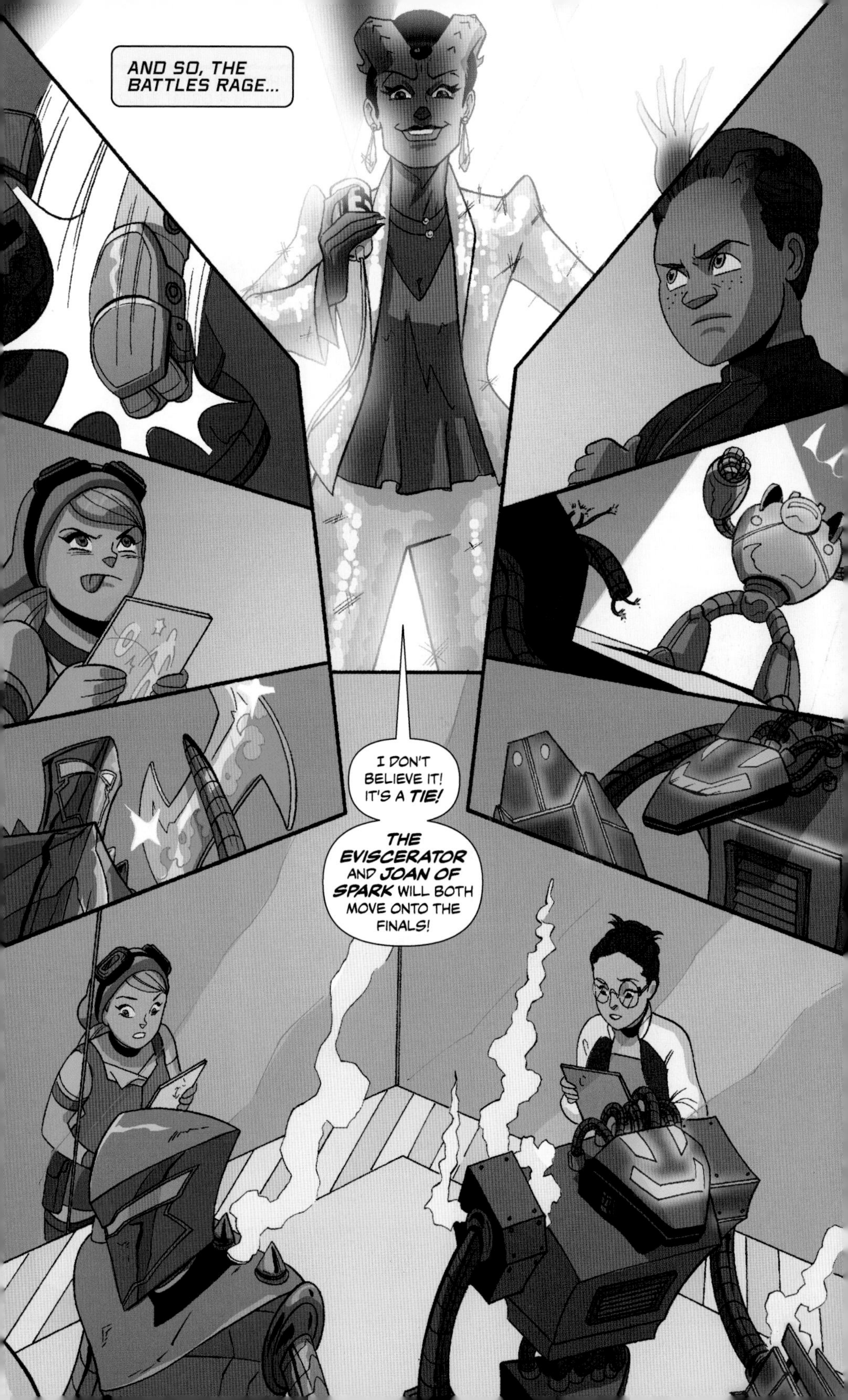
AND SO, THE BATTLES RAGE...
I DON'T BELIEVE IT! IT'S A TIE!
THE EVISCERATOR AND JOAN OF SPARK WILL BOTH MOVE ONTO THE FINALS!

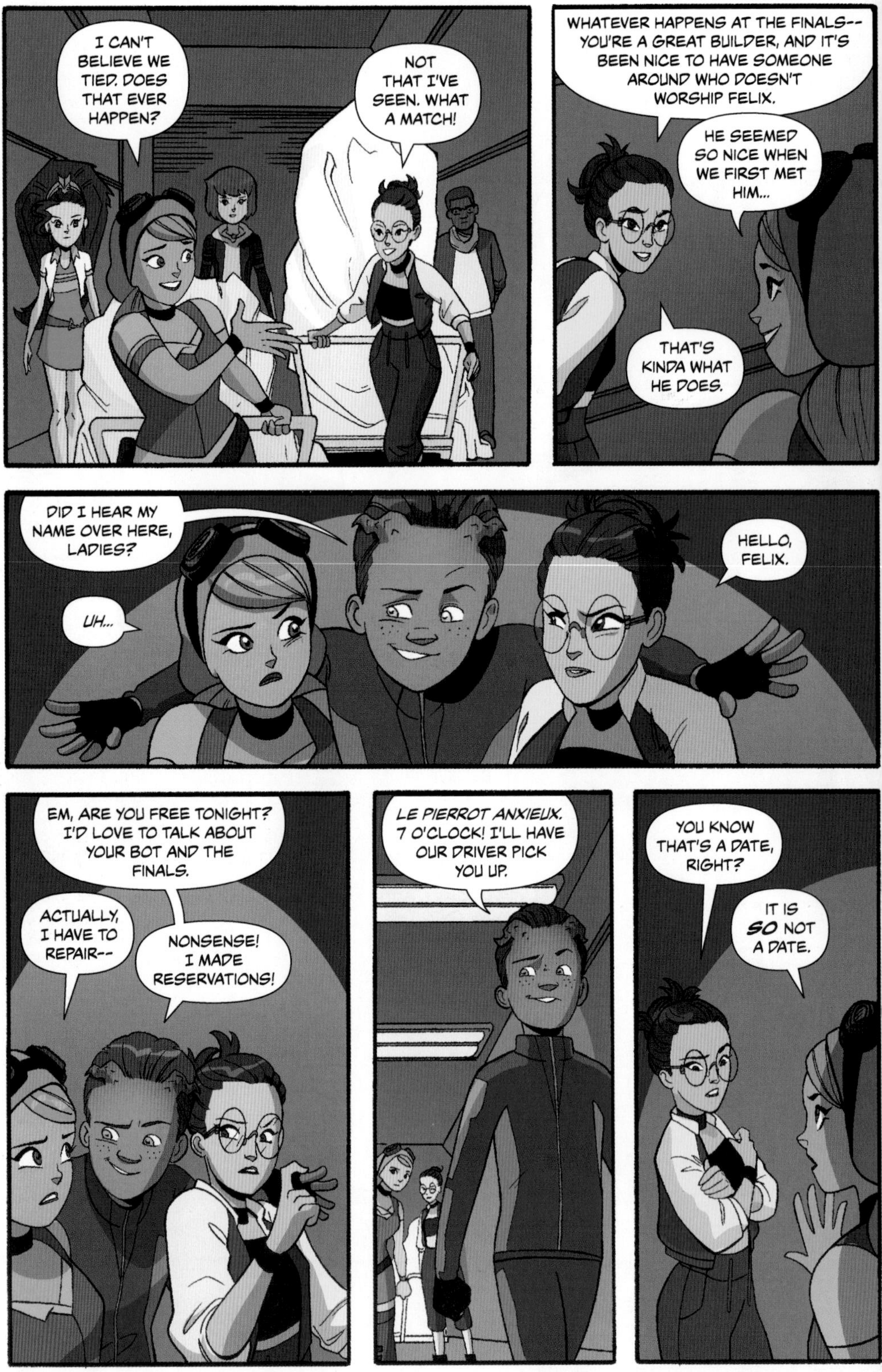
I CAN'T BELIEVE WE TIED. DOES THAT EVER HAPPEN?
NOT THAT I'VE SEEN. WHAT A MATCH!
WHATEVER HAPPENS AT THE FINALS-- YOU'RE A GREAT BUILDER, AND IT'S BEEN NICE TO HAVE SOMEONE AROUND WHO DOESN'T WORSHIP FELIX.
HE SEEMED SO NICE WHEN WE FIRST MET HIM...
THAT'S KINDA WHAT HE DOES.
DID I HEAR MY NAME OVER HERE, LADIES?
HELLO, FELIX.
UH...
EM, ARE YOU FREE TONIGHT? I'D LOVE TO TALK ABOUT YOUR BOT AND THE FINALS.
ACTUALLY, I HAVE TO REPAIR--
NONSENSE! I MADE RESERVATIONS!
LE PIERROT ANXIEUX. 7 O'CLOCK! I'LL HAVE OUR DRIVER PICK YOU UP.
YOU KNOW THAT'S A DATE, RIGHT?
IT IS SO NOT A DATE.

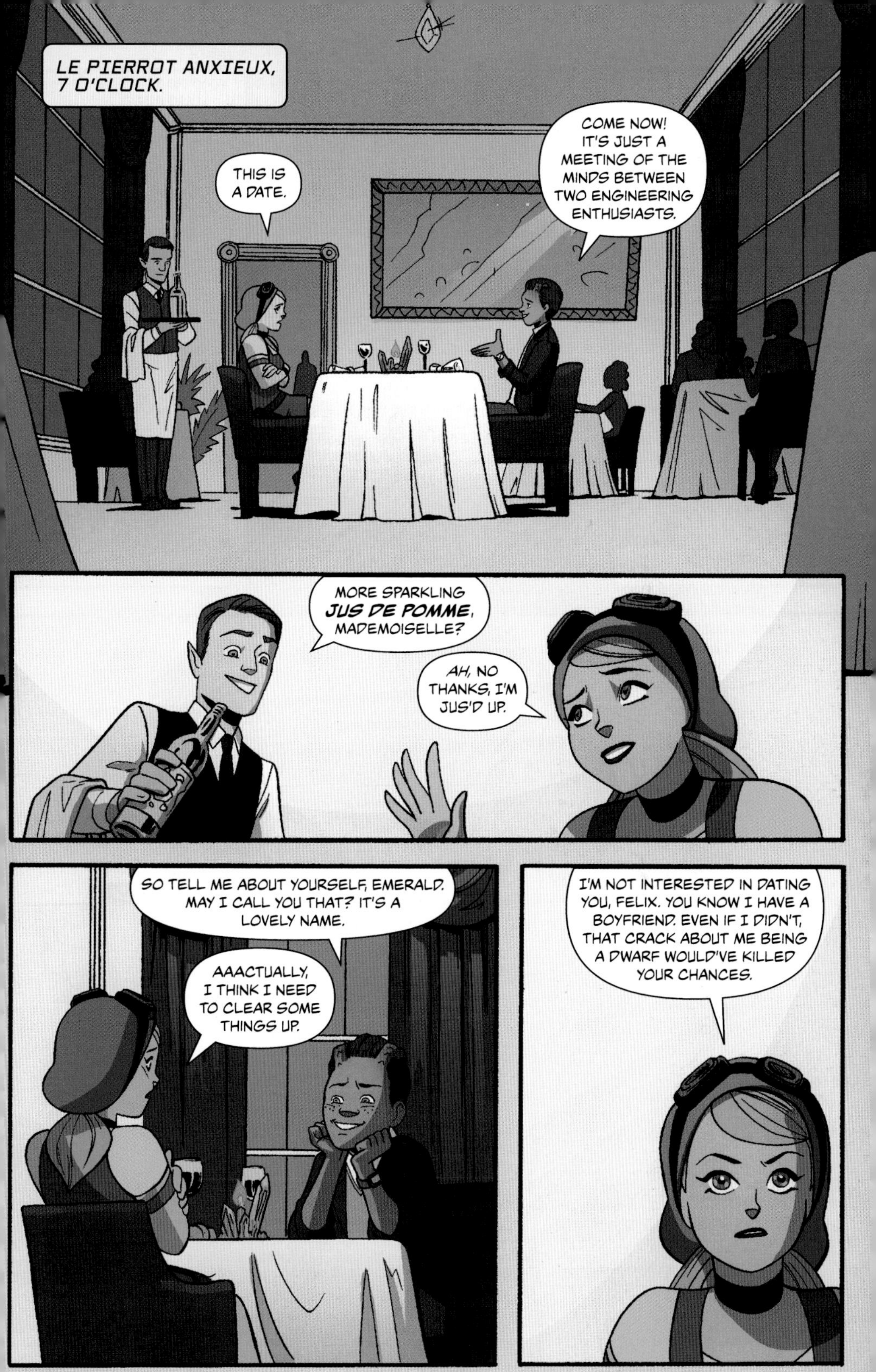
LE PIERROT ANXIEUX, 7 O'CLOCK.
THIS IS A DATE.
COME NOW! IT'S JUST A MEETING OF THE MINDS BETWEEN TWO ENGINEERING ENTHUSIASTS.
MORE SPARKLING JUS DE POMME, MADEMOISELLE?
AH, NO THANKS, I'M JUS'D UP.
SO TELL ME ABOUT YOURSELF, EMERALD. MAY I CALL YOU THAT? IT'S A LOVELY NAME.
AAACTUALLY, I THINK I NEED TO CLEAR SOME THINGS UP.
I'M NOT INTERESTED IN DATING YOU, FELIX. YOU KNOW I HAVE A BOYFRIEND. EVEN IF I DIDN'T, THAT CRACK ABOUT ME BEING A DWARF WOULD'VE KILLED YOUR CHANCES.

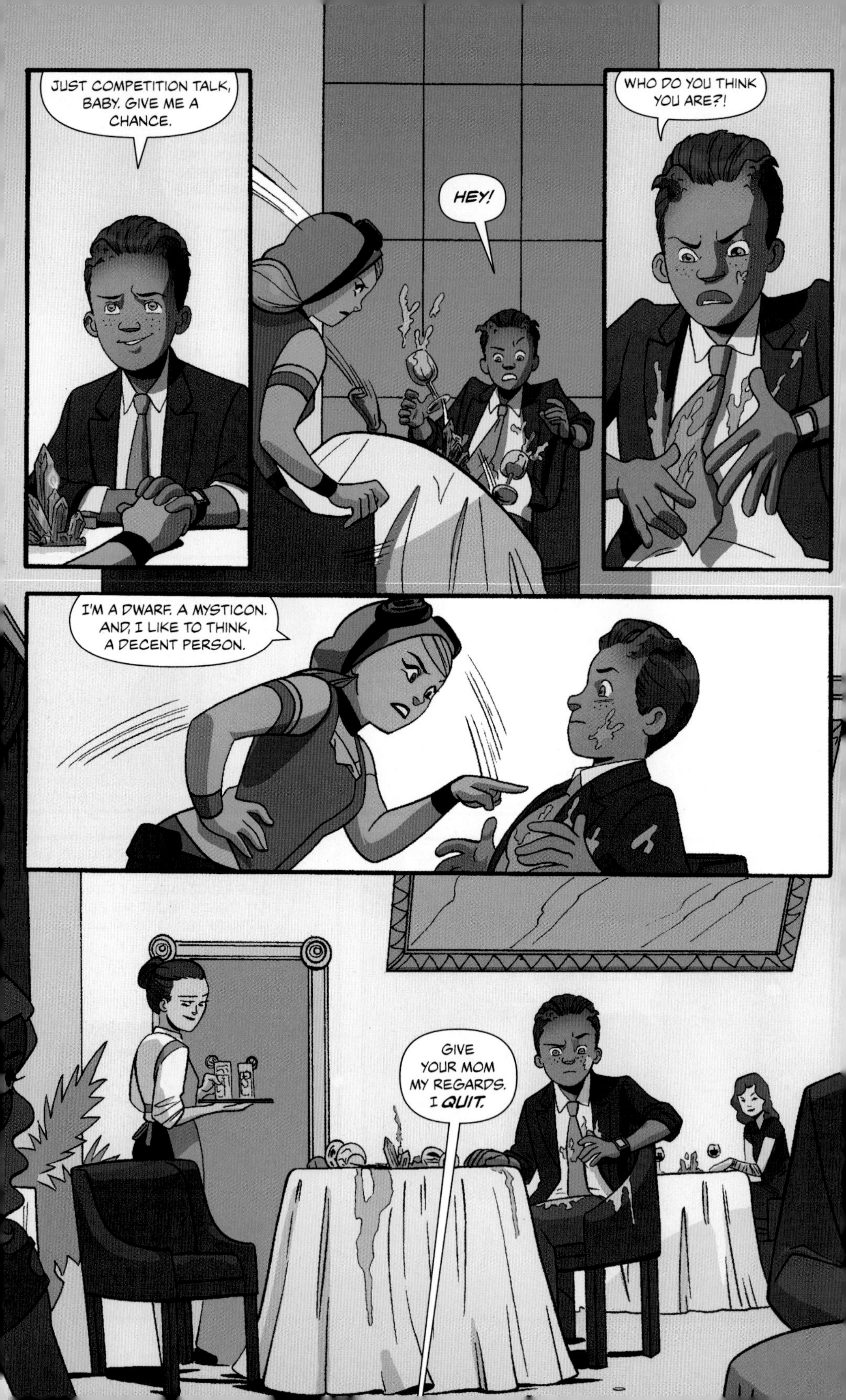
JUST COMPETITION TALK, BABY. GIVE ME A CHANCE.
HEY!
WHO DO YOU THINK YOU ARE?!
I'M A DWARF. A MYSTICON. AND, I LIKE TO THINK, A DECENT PERSON.
GIVE YOUR MOM MY REGARDS. I **QUIT.**

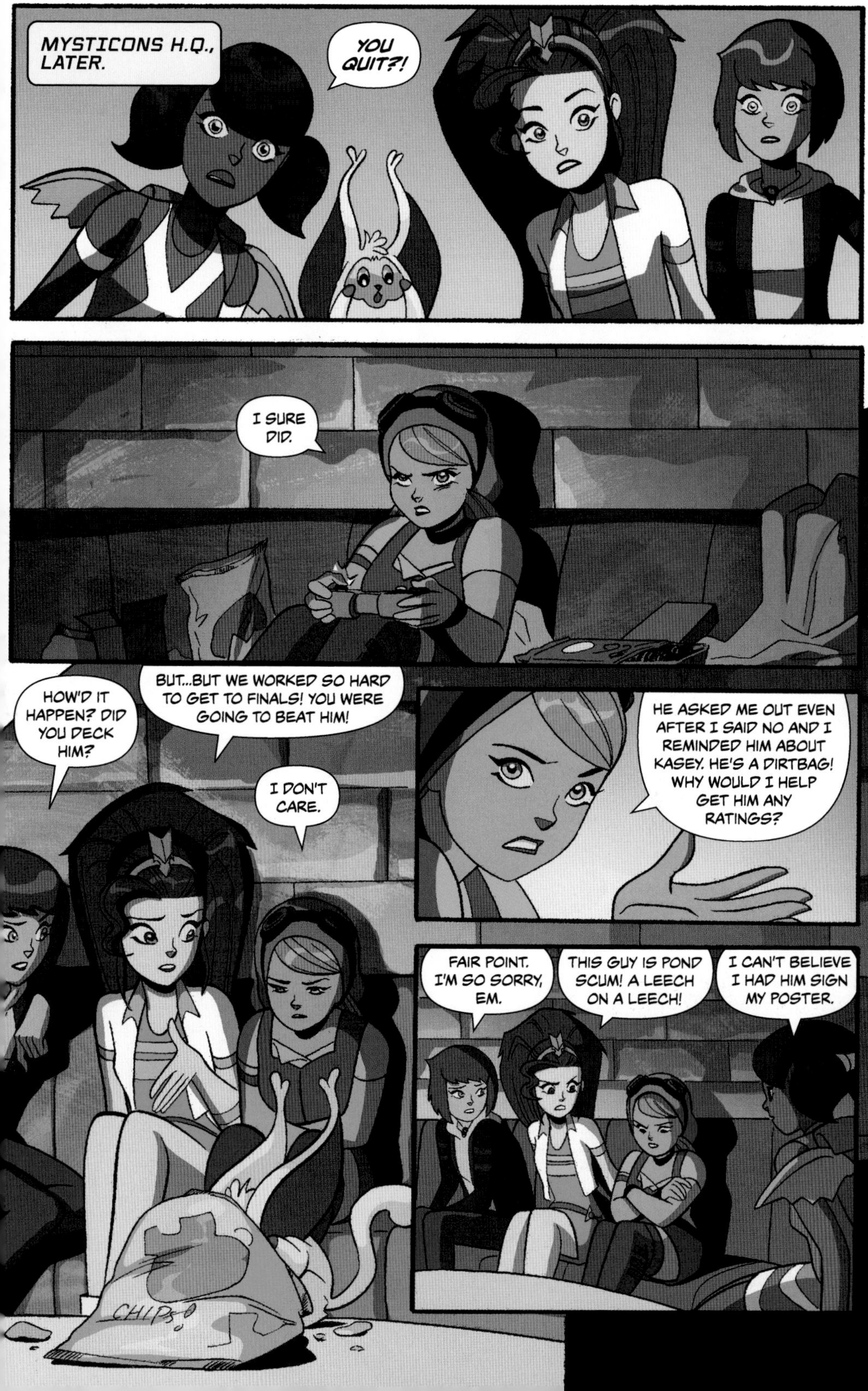
MYSTICONS H.Q., LATER.
YOU QUIT?!
I SURE DID.
HOW'D IT HAPPEN? DID YOU DECK HIM?
BUT...BUT WE WORKED SO HARD TO GET TO FINALS! YOU WERE GOING TO BEAT HIM!
I DON'T CARE.
HE ASKED ME OUT EVEN AFTER I SAID NO AND I REMINDED HIM ABOUT KASEY. HE'S A DIRTBAG! WHY WOULD I HELP GET HIM ANY RATINGS?
FAIR POINT. I'M SO SORRY, EM.
THIS GUY IS POND SCUM! A LEECH ON A LEECH!
I CAN'T BELIEVE I HAD HIM SIGN MY POSTER.
CHIPS

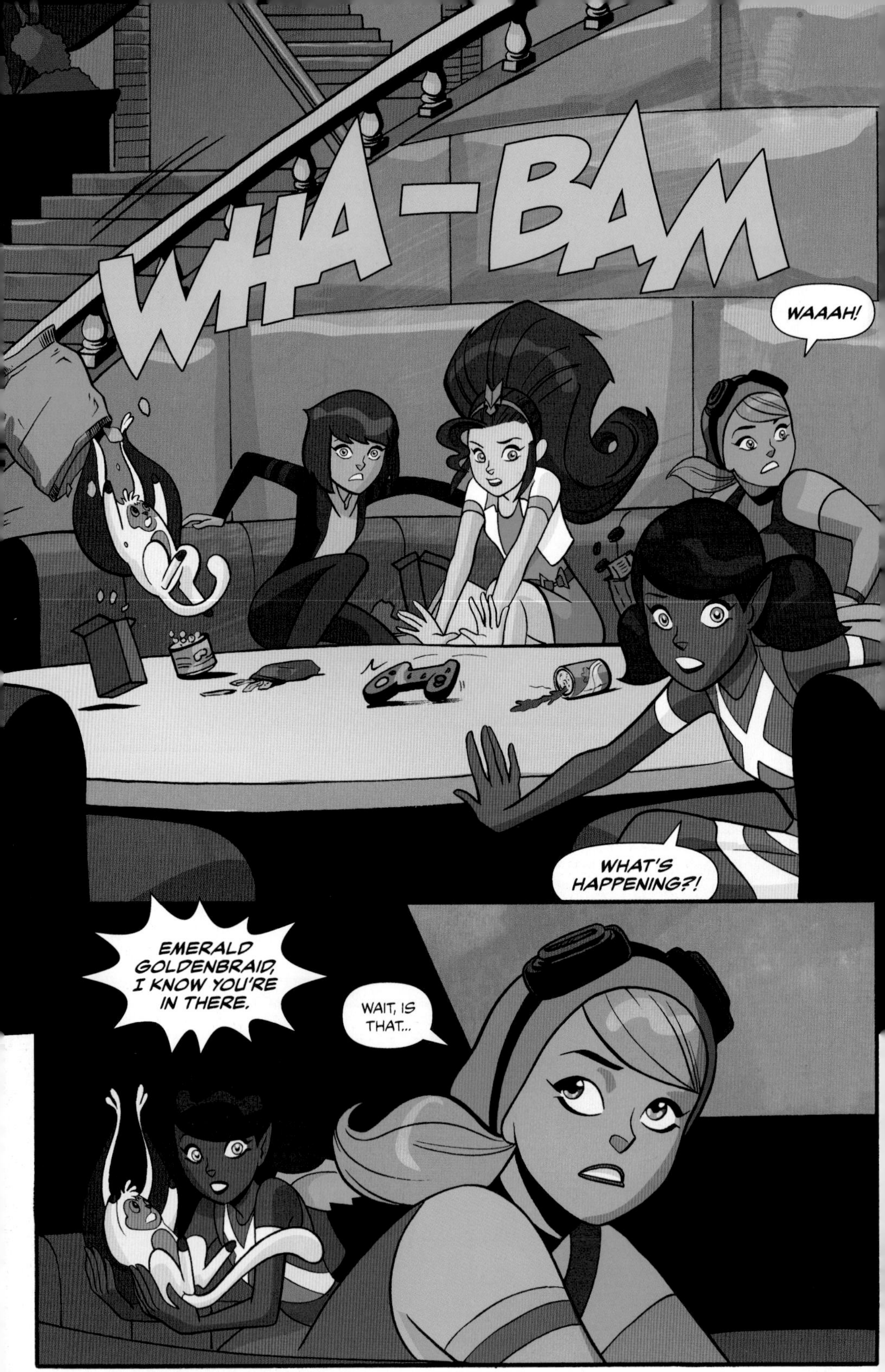
WHA-BAM
WAAAH!
WHAT'S HAPPENING?!
EMERALD GOLDENBRAID, I KNOW YOU'RE IN THERE.
WAIT, IS THAT...

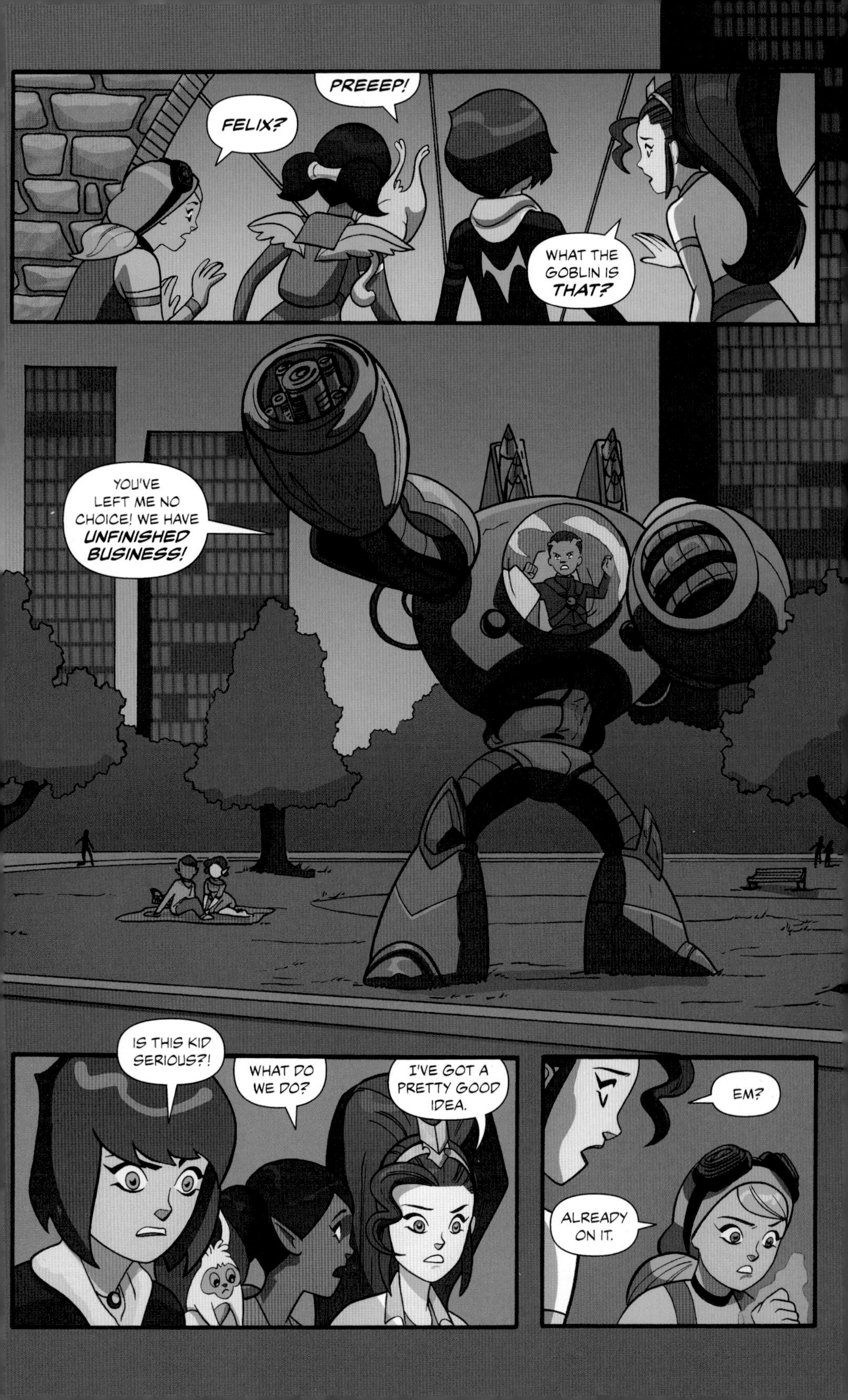
FELIX?
PREEEP!
WHAT THE GOBLIN IS THAT?
YOU'VE LEFT ME NO CHOICE! WE HAVE UNFINISHED BUSINESS!
IS THIS KID SERIOUS?!
WHAT DO WE DO?
I'VE GOT A PRETTY GOOD IDEA.
EM?
ALREADY ON IT.

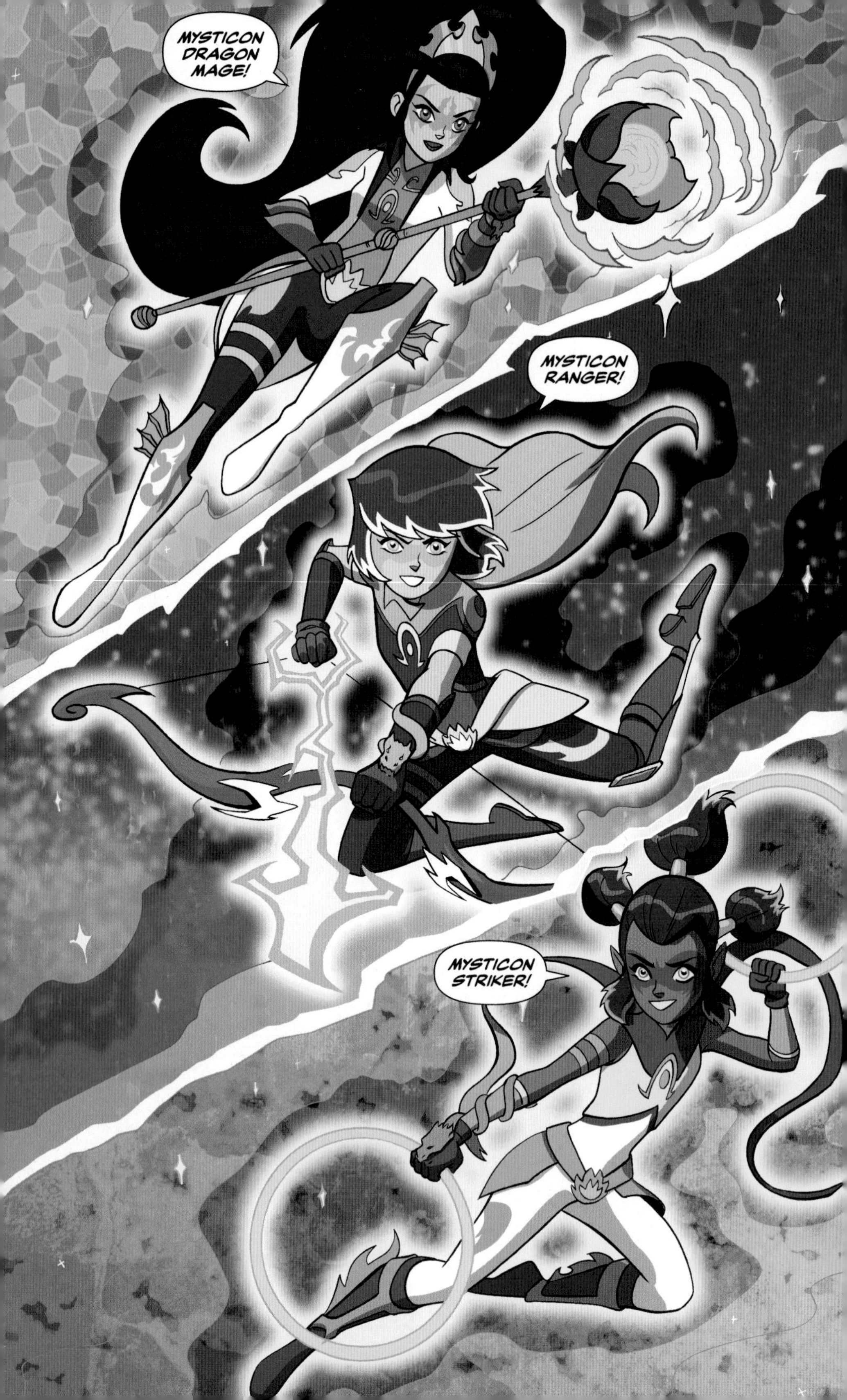
MYSTICON DRAGON MAGE!
MYSTICON RANGER!
MYSTICON STRIKER!

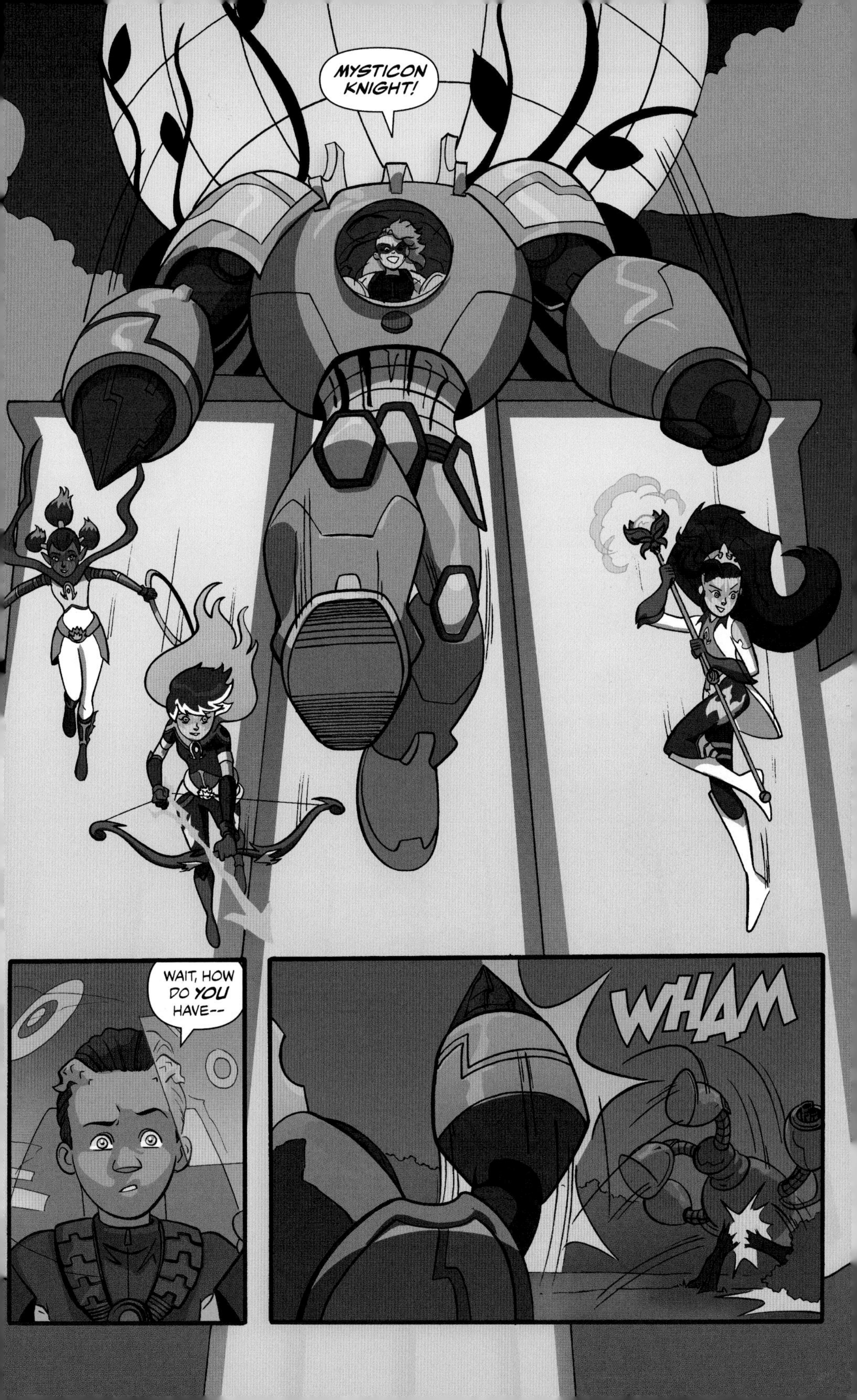
MYSTICON KNIGHT!
WAIT, HOW DO YOU HAVE--
WHAM

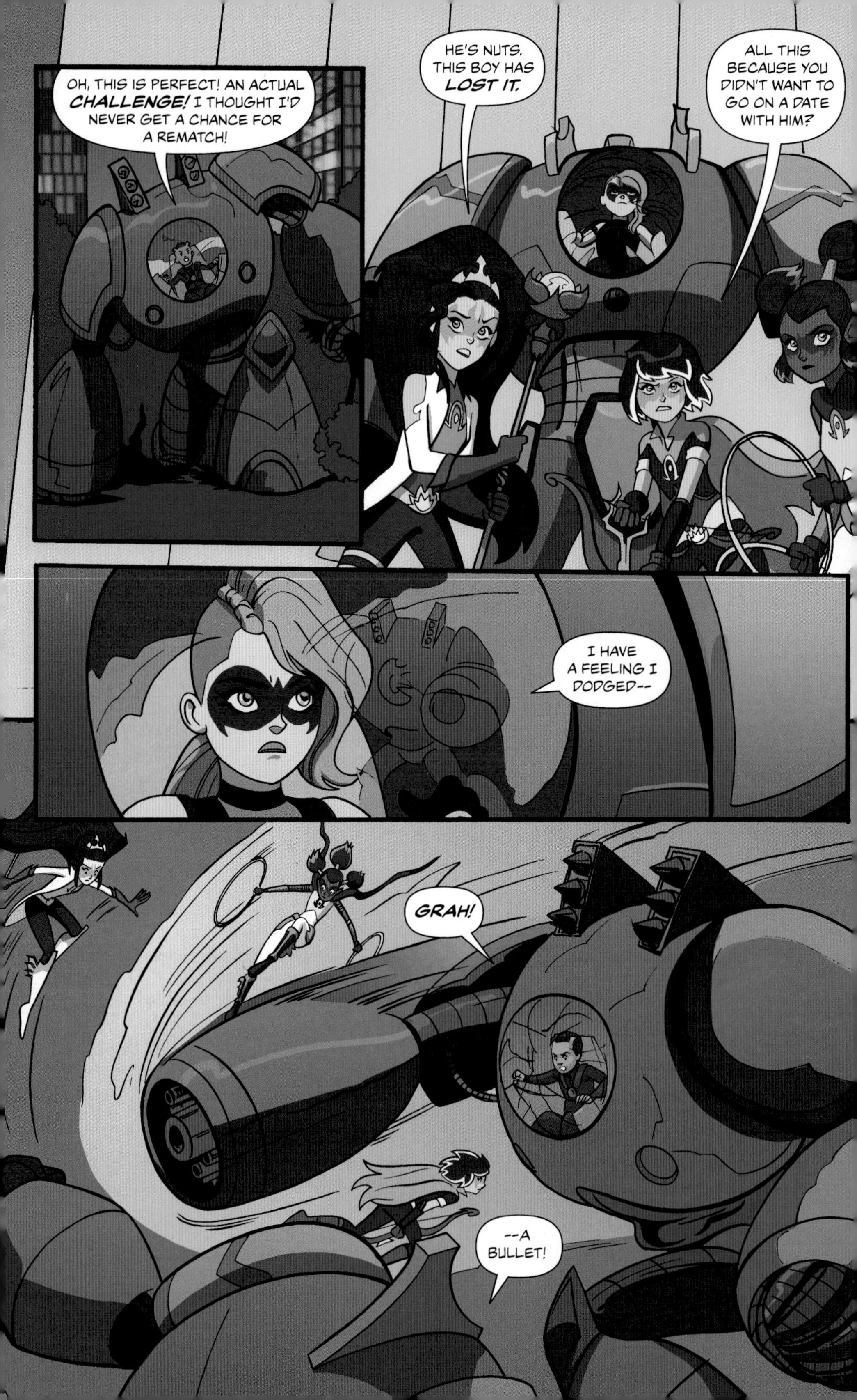
OH, THIS IS PERFECT! AN ACTUAL *CHALLENGE!* I THOUGHT I'D NEVER GET A CHANCE FOR A REMATCH!
HE'S NUTS. THIS BOY HAS *LOST IT.*
ALL THIS BECAUSE YOU DIDN'T WANT TO GO ON A DATE WITH HIM?
I HAVE A FEELING I DODGED--
GRAH!
--A BULLET!

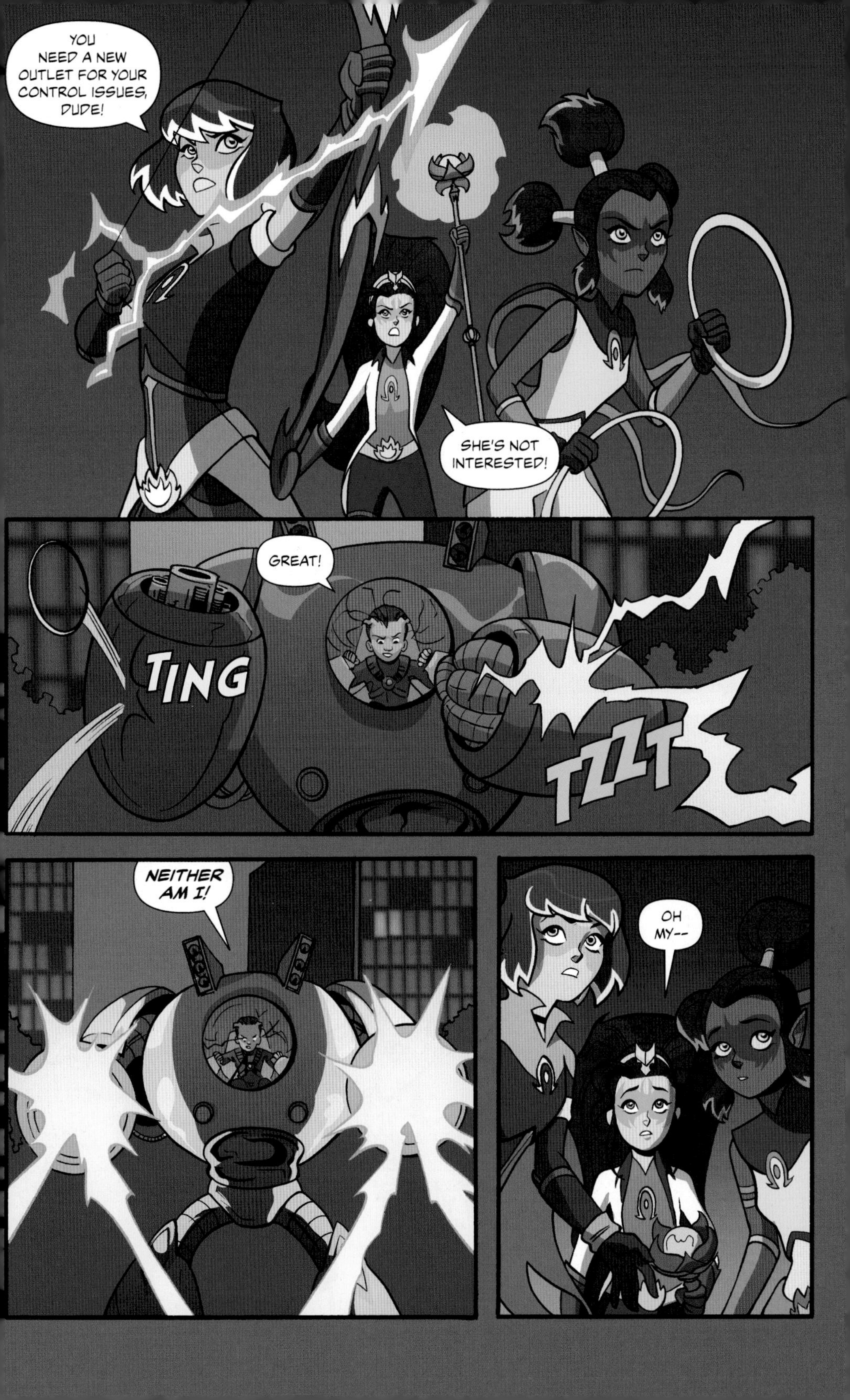
YOU NEED A NEW OUTLET FOR YOUR CONTROL ISSUES, DUDE!
SHE'S NOT INTERESTED!
GREAT!
TING
TZZT
NEITHER AM I!
OH MY--

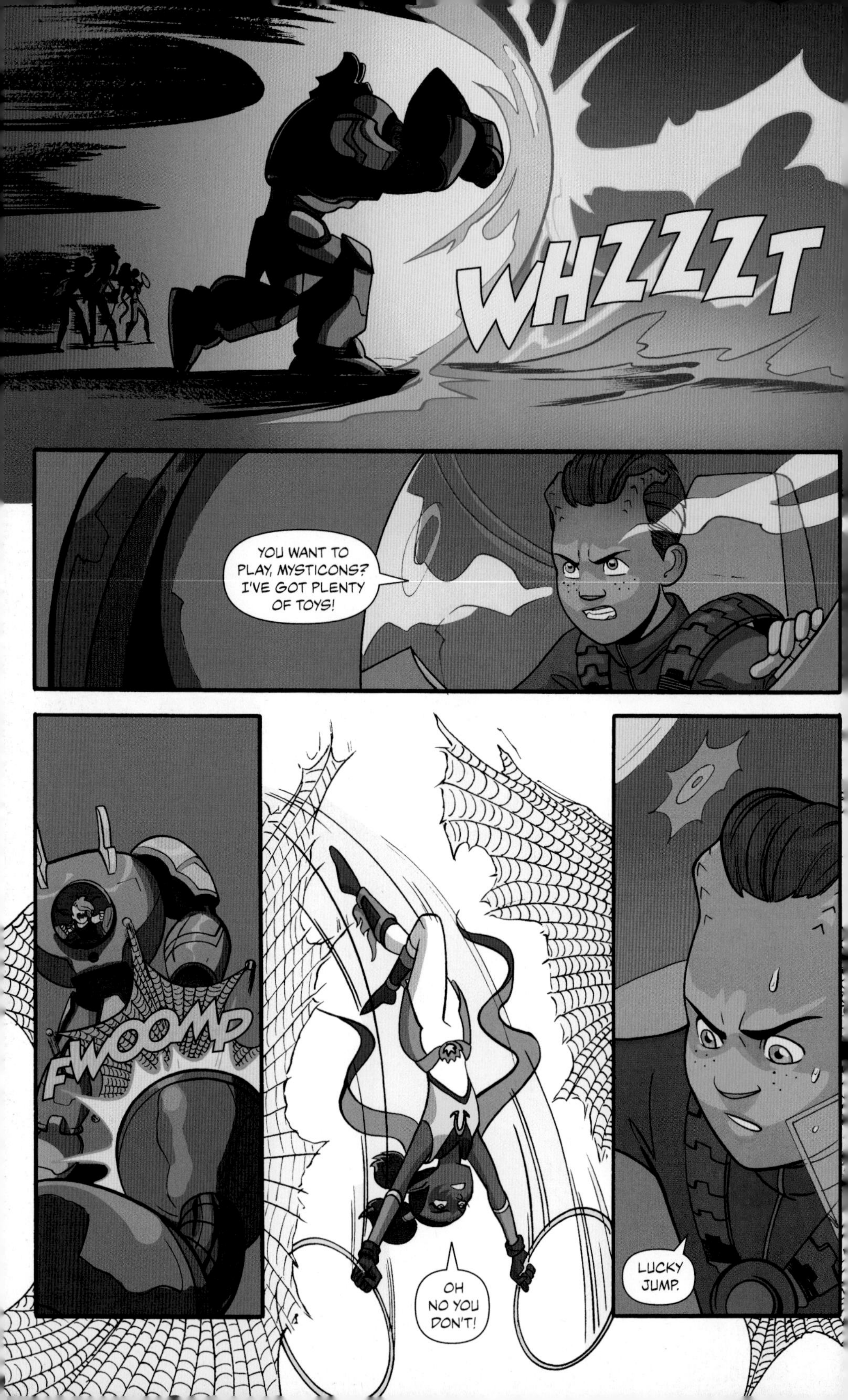
WHZZZT
YOU WANT TO PLAY, MYSTICONS? I'VE GOT PLENTY OF TOYS!
FWOOMP
OH NO YOU DON'T!
LUCKY JUMP.

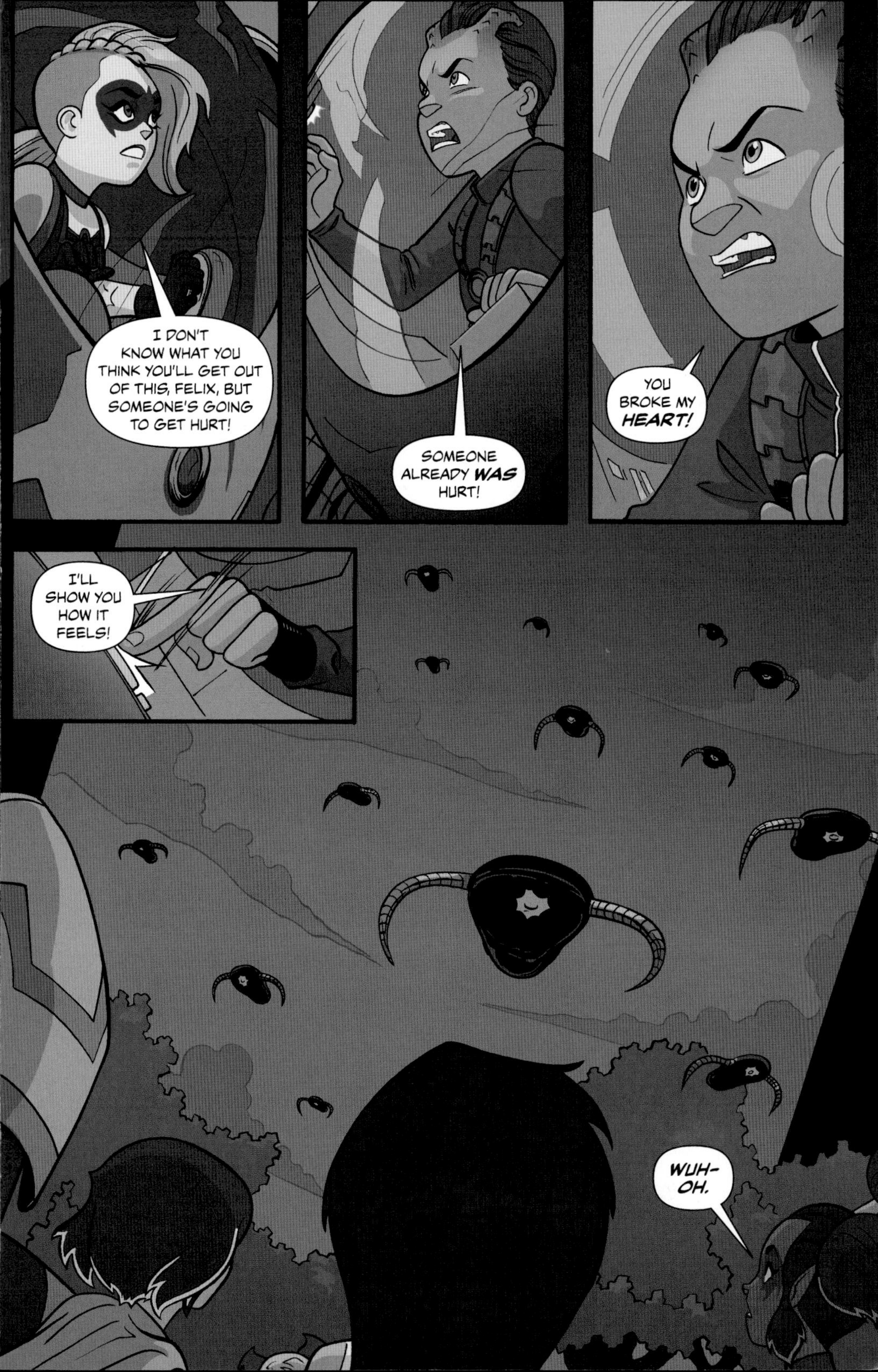

I DON'T KNOW WHAT YOU THINK YOU'LL GET OUT OF THIS, FELIX, BUT SOMEONE'S GOING TO GET HURT!
SOMEONE ALREADY **WAS** HURT!
YOU BROKE MY **HEART!**
I'LL SHOW YOU HOW IT FEELS!
WUH-OH.

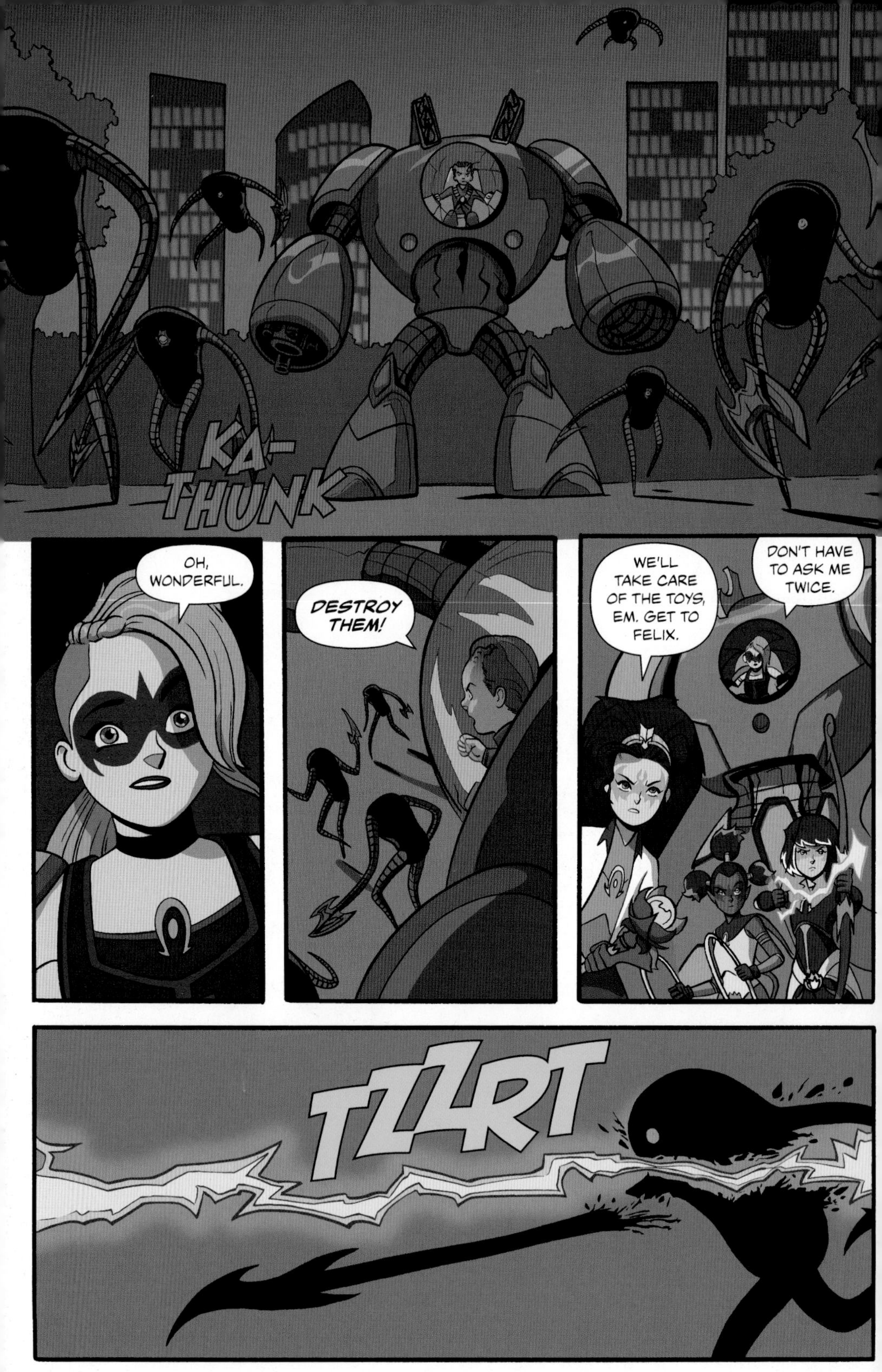
KA-THUNK
OH, WONDERFUL.
DESTROY THEM!
WE'LL TAKE CARE OF THE TOYS, EM. GET TO FELIX.
DON'T HAVE TO ASK ME TWICE.
TZZRT

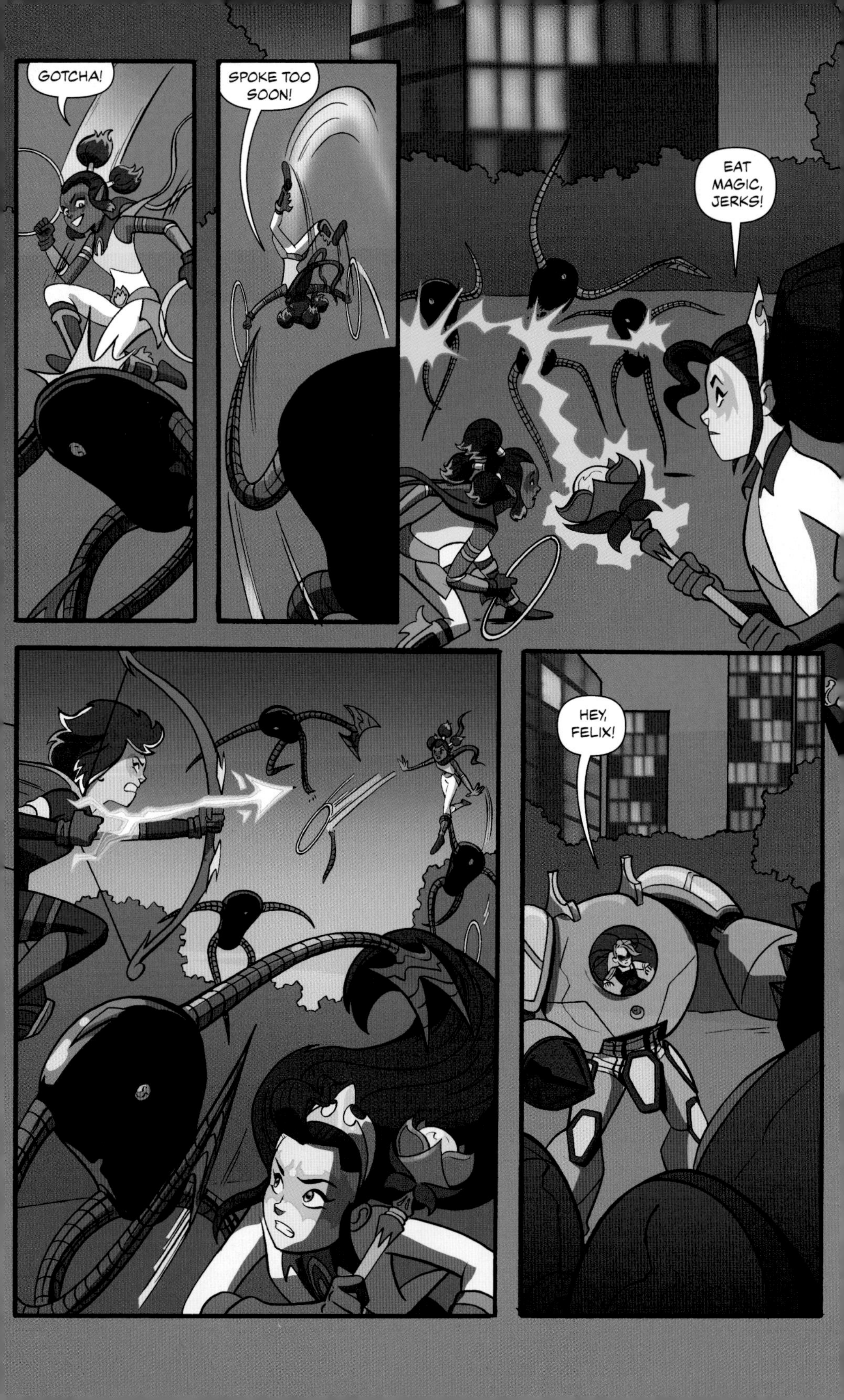
GOTCHA!
SPOKE TOO SOON!
EAT MAGIC, JERKS!
HEY, FELIX!

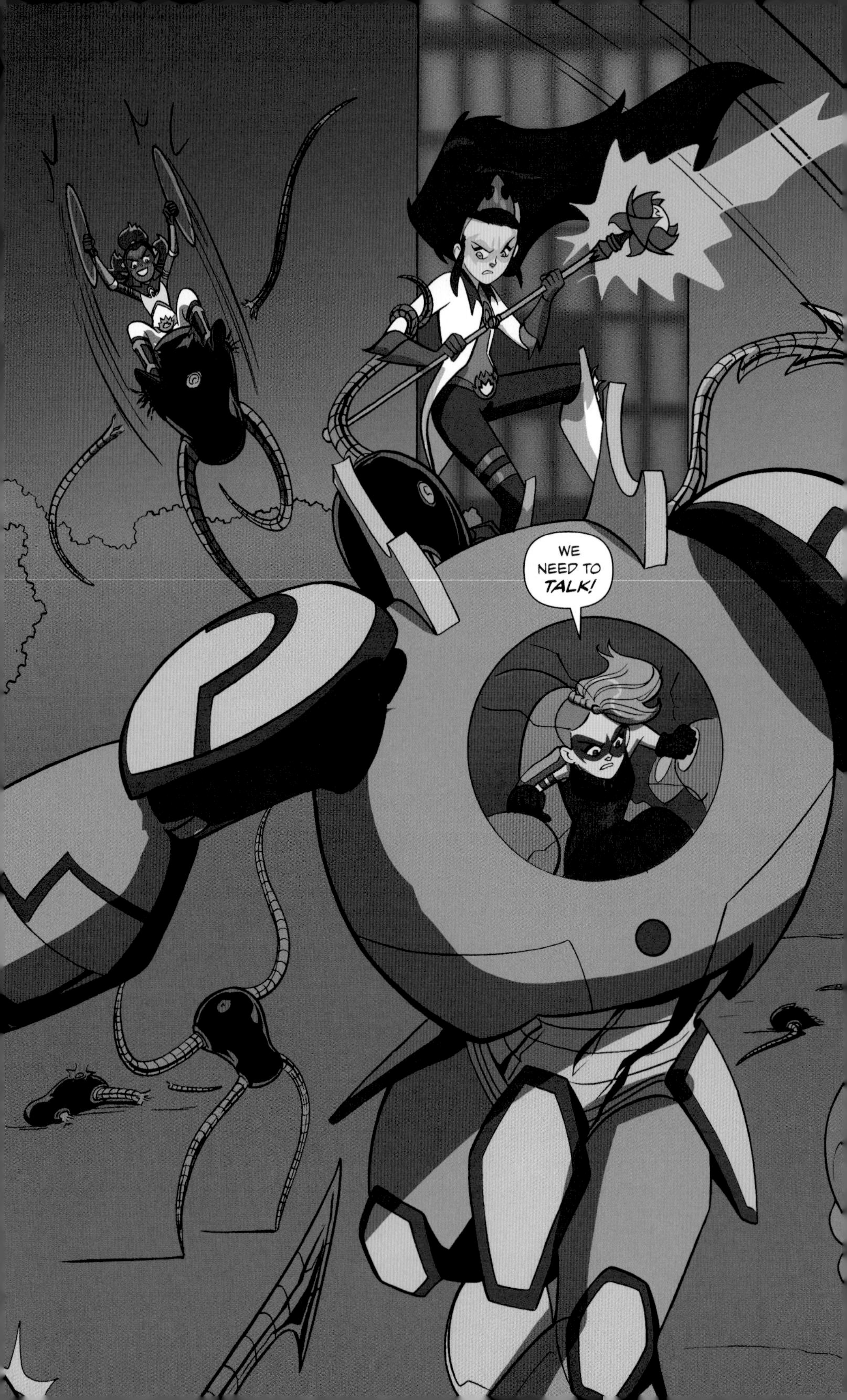
WE NEED TO TALK!

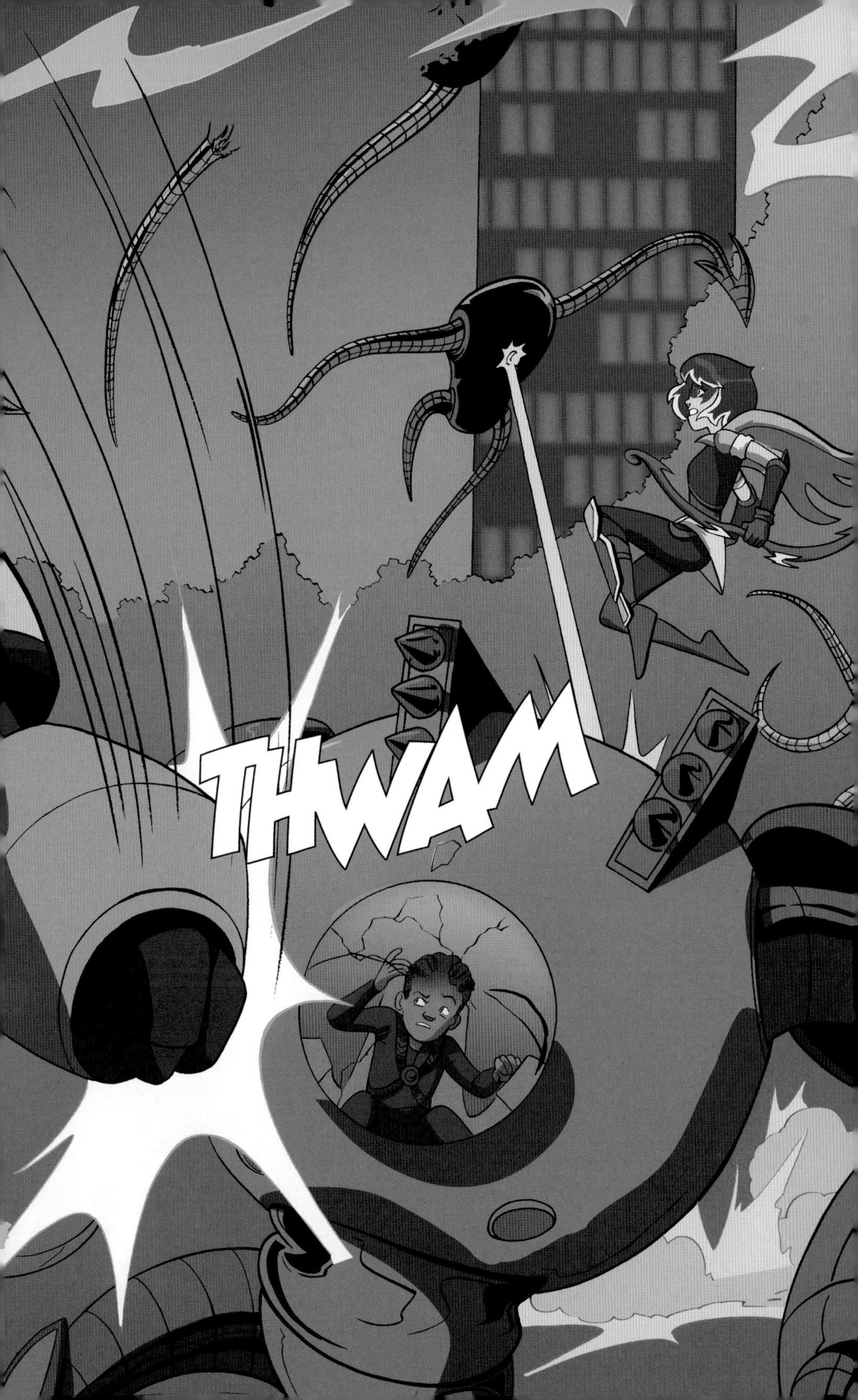
THWAM

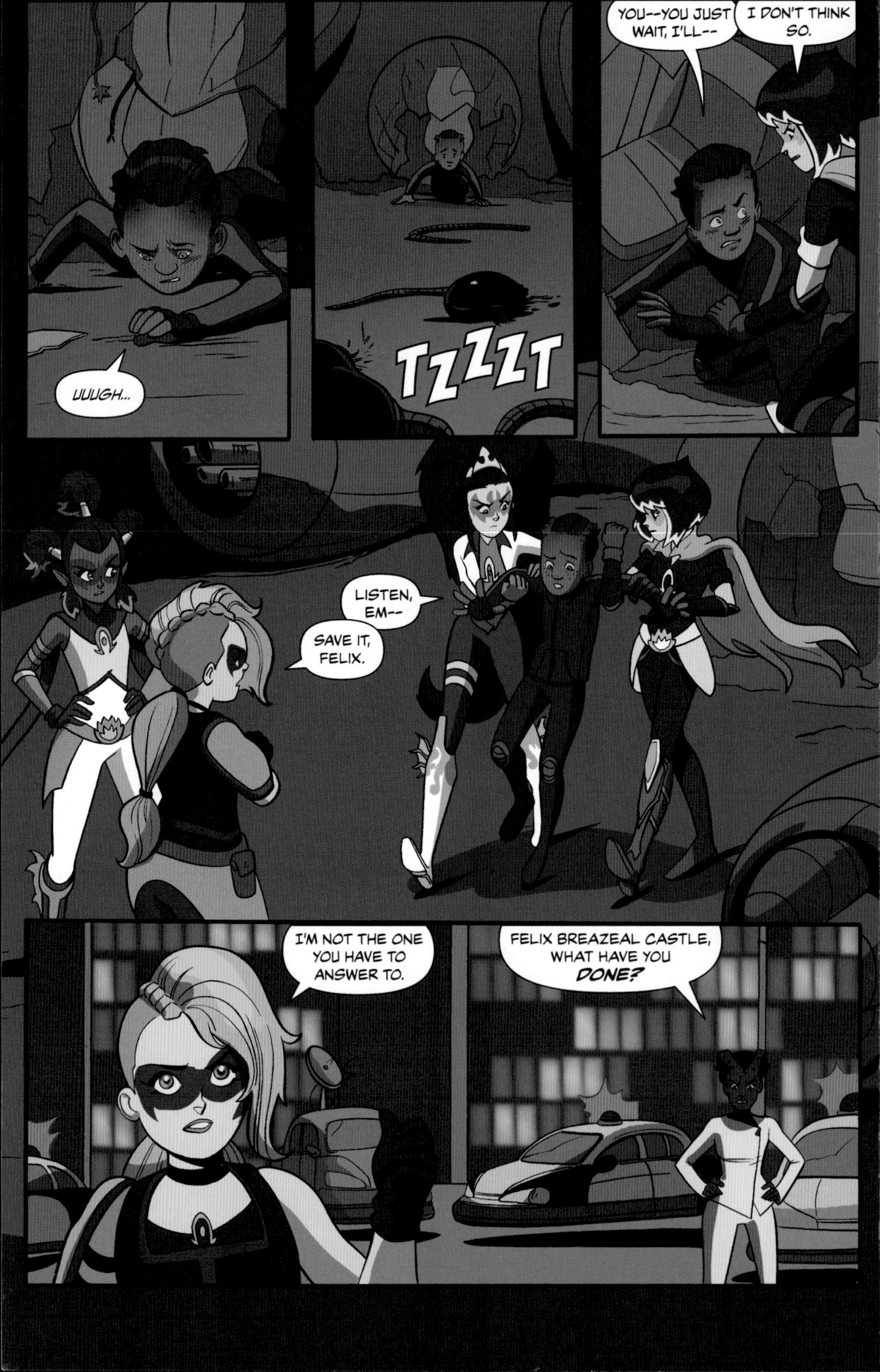
UUUGH...
TZZZT
YOU--YOU JUST WAIT, I'LL--
I DON'T THINK SO.
LISTEN, EM--
SAVE IT, FELIX.
I'M NOT THE ONE YOU HAVE TO ANSWER TO.
FELIX BREAZEAL CASTLE, WHAT HAVE YOU *DONE?*

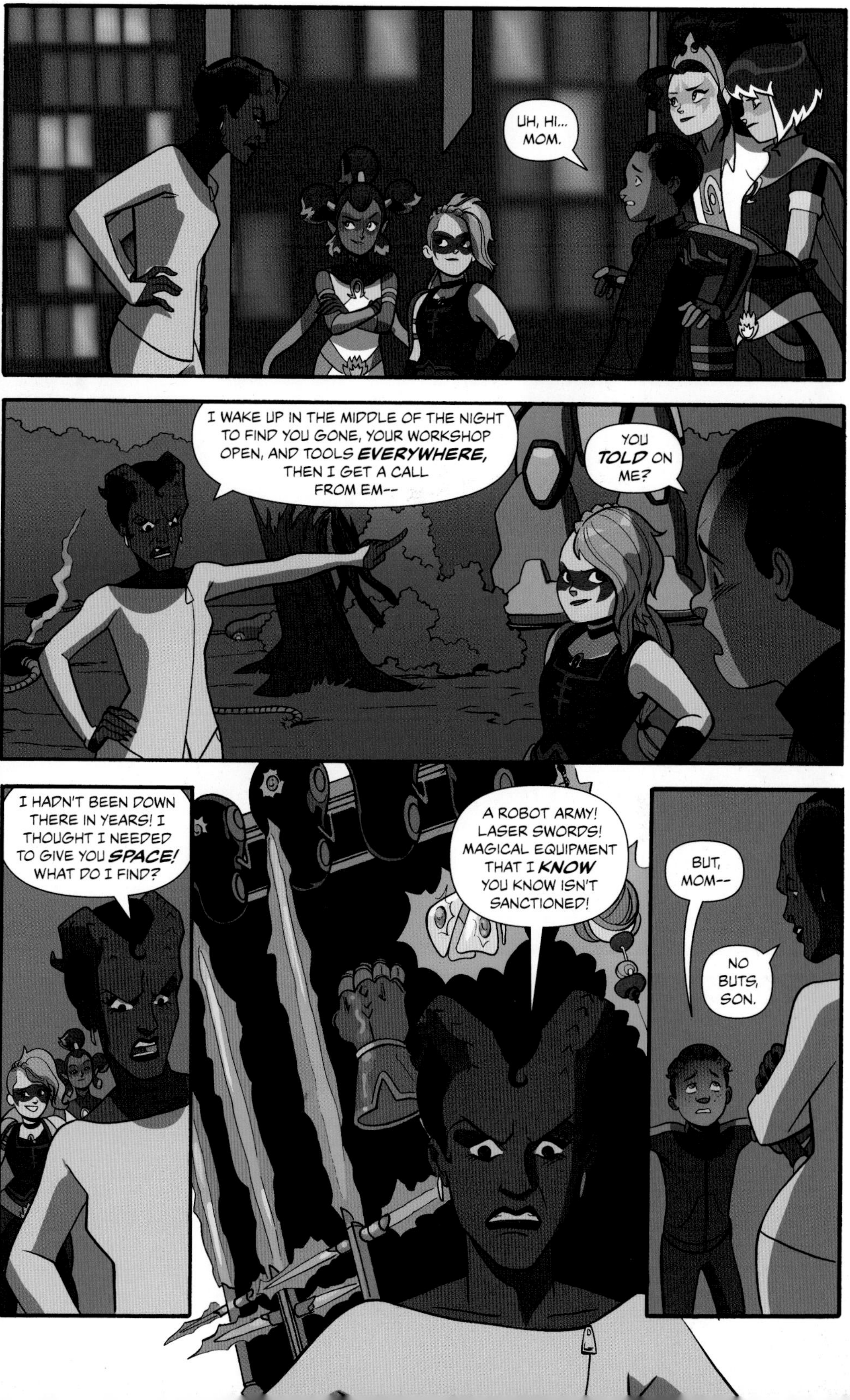
UH, HI... MOM.
I WAKE UP IN THE MIDDLE OF THE NIGHT TO FIND YOU GONE, YOUR WORKSHOP OPEN, AND TOOLS **EVERYWHERE,** THEN I GET A CALL FROM EM--
YOU **TOLD** ON ME?
I HADN'T BEEN DOWN THERE IN YEARS! I THOUGHT I NEEDED TO GIVE YOU **SPACE!** WHAT DO I FIND?
A ROBOT ARMY! LASER SWORDS! MAGICAL EQUIPMENT THAT I **KNOW** YOU KNOW ISN'T SANCTIONED!
BUT, MOM--
NO BUTS, SON.

YOU'RE GROUNDED.

SAY CHEESE, FELIX.

KLIK

I CAN'T BELIEVE THIS. I'M SO SORRY. THIS IS GOING TO BE A LEGAL MESS... I'LL BE LUCKY IF THE WHOLE SHOW DOESN'T GO UNDER.

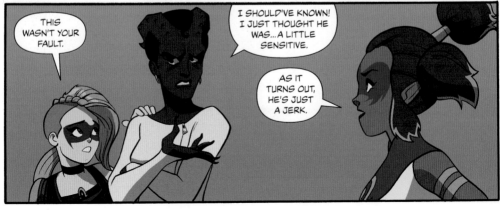

THIS WASN'T YOUR FAULT.

I SHOULD'VE KNOWN! I JUST THOUGHT HE WAS... A LITTLE SENSITIVE.

AS IT TURNS OUT, HE'S JUST A JERK.

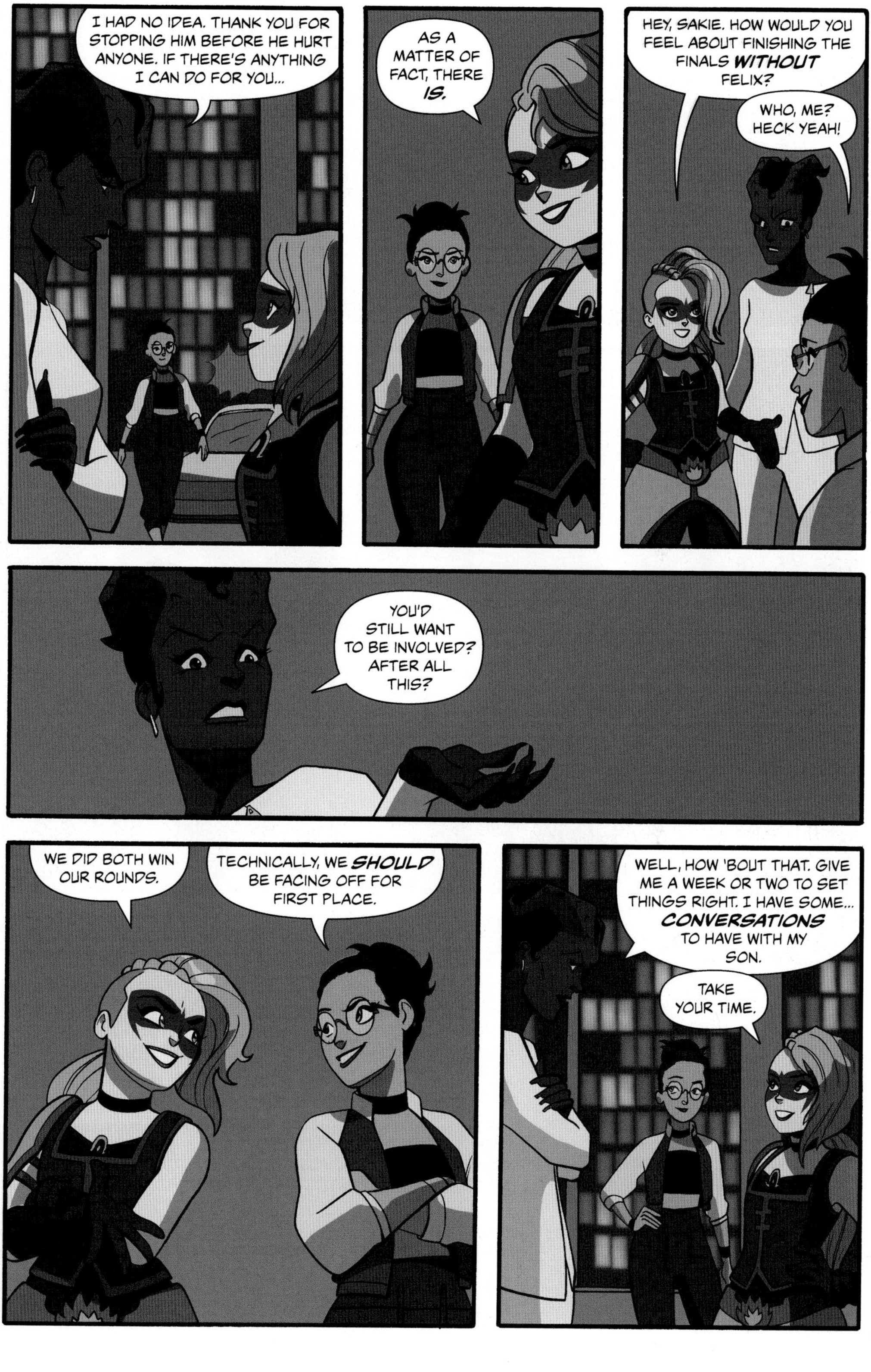
I HAD NO IDEA. THANK YOU FOR STOPPING HIM BEFORE HE HURT ANYONE. IF THERE'S ANYTHING I CAN DO FOR YOU...
AS A MATTER OF FACT, THERE *IS.*
HEY, SAKIE. HOW WOULD YOU FEEL ABOUT FINISHING THE FINALS ***WITHOUT*** FELIX?
WHO, ME? HECK YEAH!
YOU'D STILL WANT TO BE INVOLVED? AFTER ALL THIS?
WE DID BOTH WIN OUR ROUNDS.
TECHNICALLY, WE ***SHOULD*** BE FACING OFF FOR FIRST PLACE.
WELL, HOW 'BOUT THAT. GIVE ME A WEEK OR TWO TO SET THINGS RIGHT. I HAVE SOME... ***CONVERSATIONS*** TO HAVE WITH MY SON.
TAKE YOUR TIME.

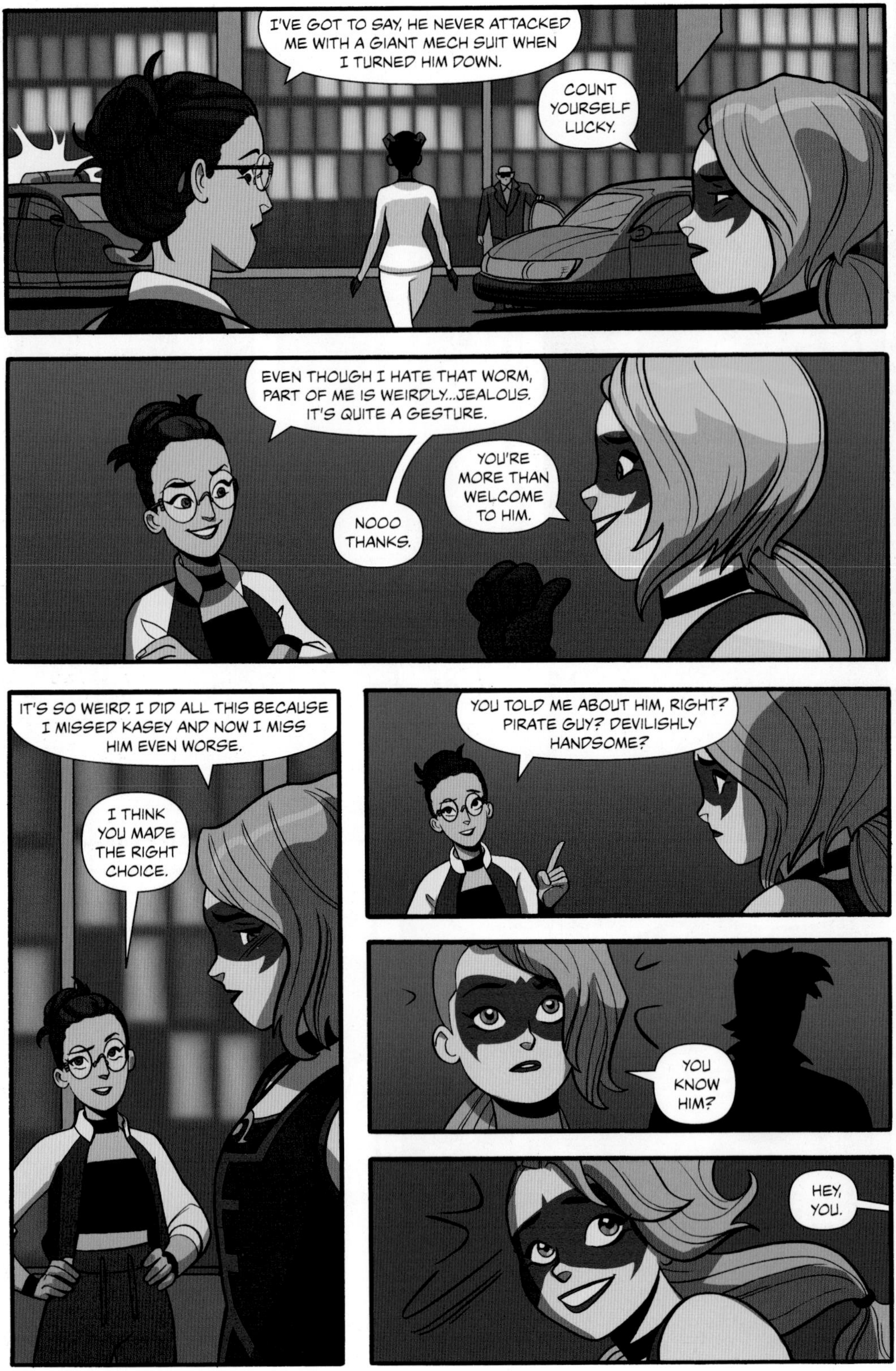
I'VE GOT TO SAY, HE NEVER ATTACKED ME WITH A GIANT MECH SUIT WHEN I TURNED HIM DOWN.
COUNT YOURSELF LUCKY.
EVEN THOUGH I HATE THAT WORM, PART OF ME IS WEIRDLY...JEALOUS. IT'S QUITE A GESTURE.
YOU'RE MORE THAN WELCOME TO HIM.
NOOO THANKS.
IT'S SO WEIRD. I DID ALL THIS BECAUSE I MISSED KASEY AND NOW I MISS HIM EVEN WORSE.
I THINK YOU MADE THE RIGHT CHOICE.
YOU TOLD ME ABOUT HIM, RIGHT? PIRATE GUY? DEVILISHLY HANDSOME?
YOU KNOW HIM?
HEY, YOU.

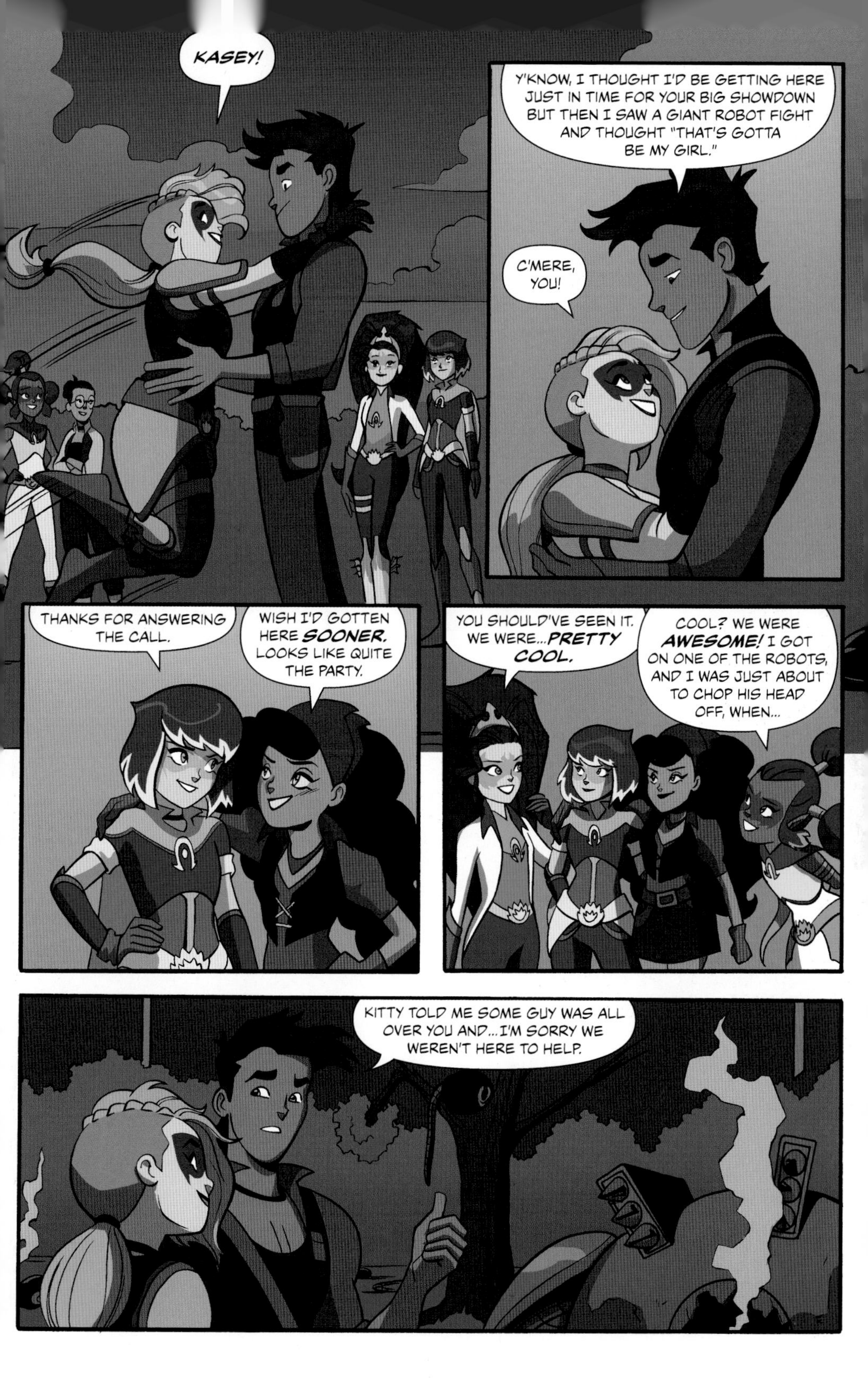
KASEY!
Y'KNOW, I THOUGHT I'D BE GETTING HERE JUST IN TIME FOR YOUR BIG SHOWDOWN BUT THEN I SAW A GIANT ROBOT FIGHT AND THOUGHT "THAT'S GOTTA BE MY GIRL."
C'MERE, YOU!
THANKS FOR ANSWERING THE CALL.
WISH I'D GOTTEN HERE SOONER. LOOKS LIKE QUITE THE PARTY.
YOU SHOULD'VE SEEN IT. WE WERE...PRETTY COOL.
COOL? WE WERE AWESOME! I GOT ON ONE OF THE ROBOTS, AND I WAS JUST ABOUT TO CHOP HIS HEAD OFF, WHEN...
KITTY TOLD ME SOME GUY WAS ALL OVER YOU AND...I'M SORRY WE WEREN'T HERE TO HELP.

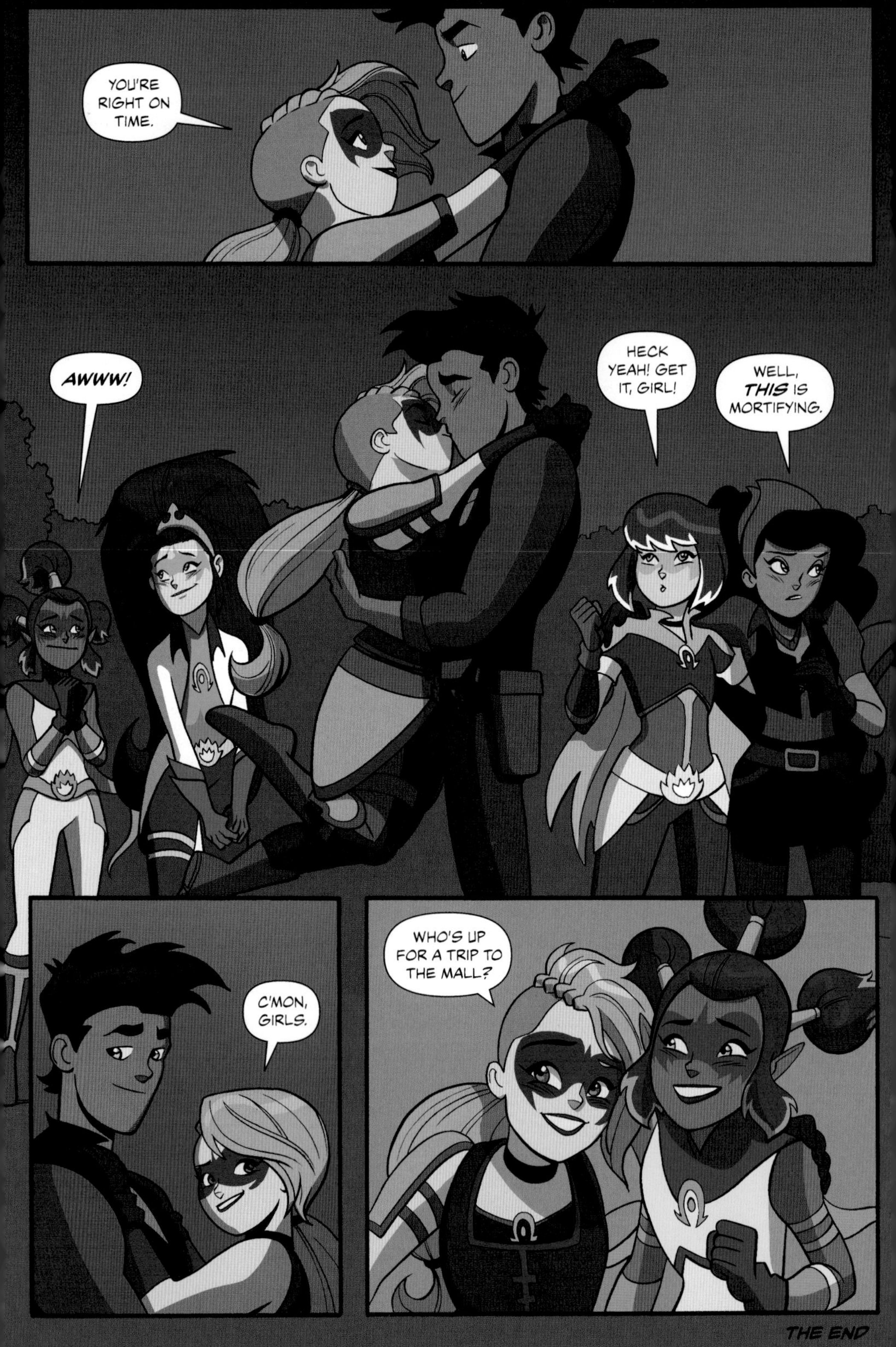
YOU'RE RIGHT ON TIME.
AWWW!
HECK YEAH! GET IT, GIRL!
WELL, THIS IS MORTIFYING.
C'MON, GIRLS.
WHO'S UP FOR A TRIP TO THE MALL?
THE END

MYSTICONS™

SKETCHBOOK

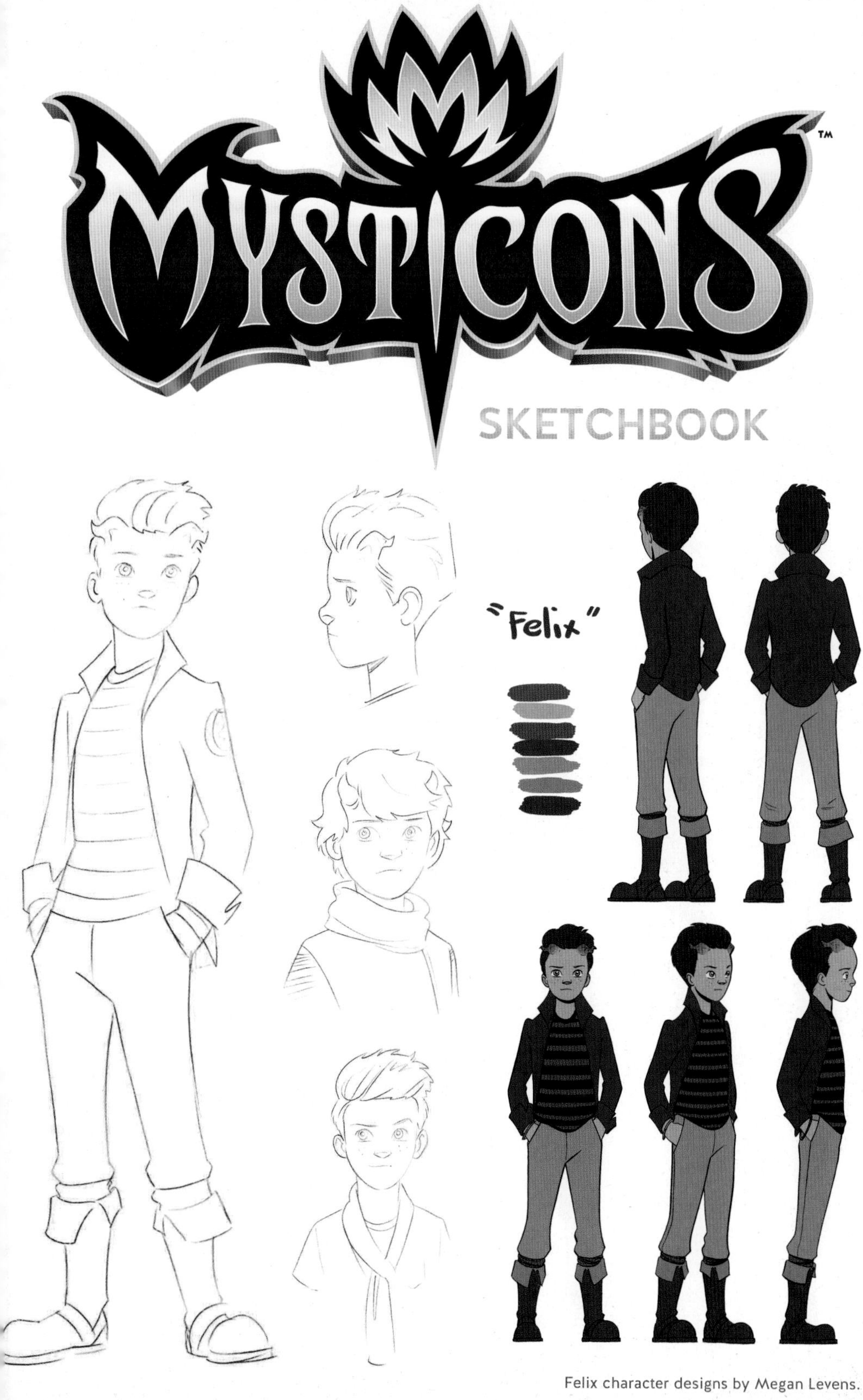
"Felix"

Felix character designs by Megan Levens.

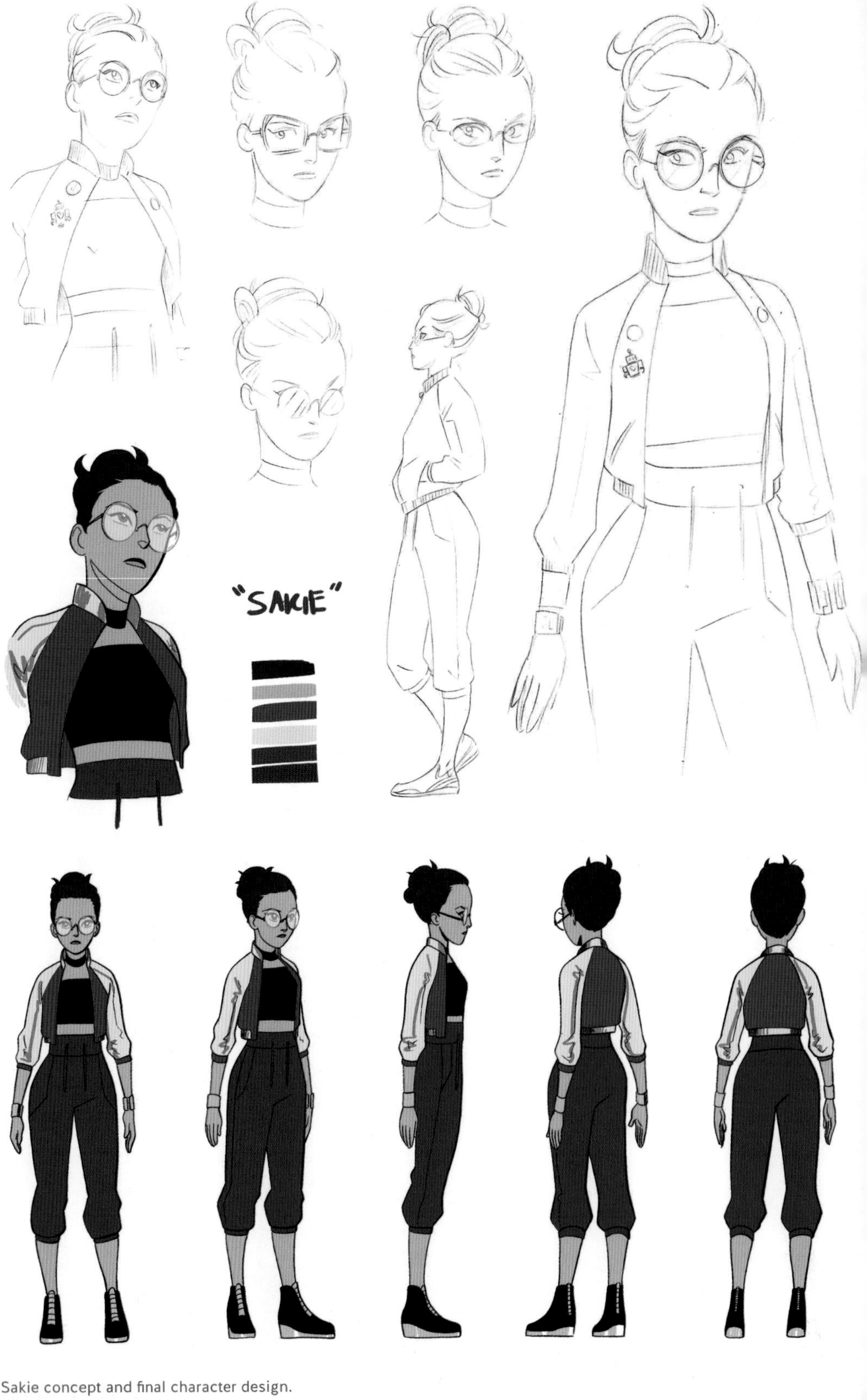
"SAKIE"

Sakie concept and final character design.

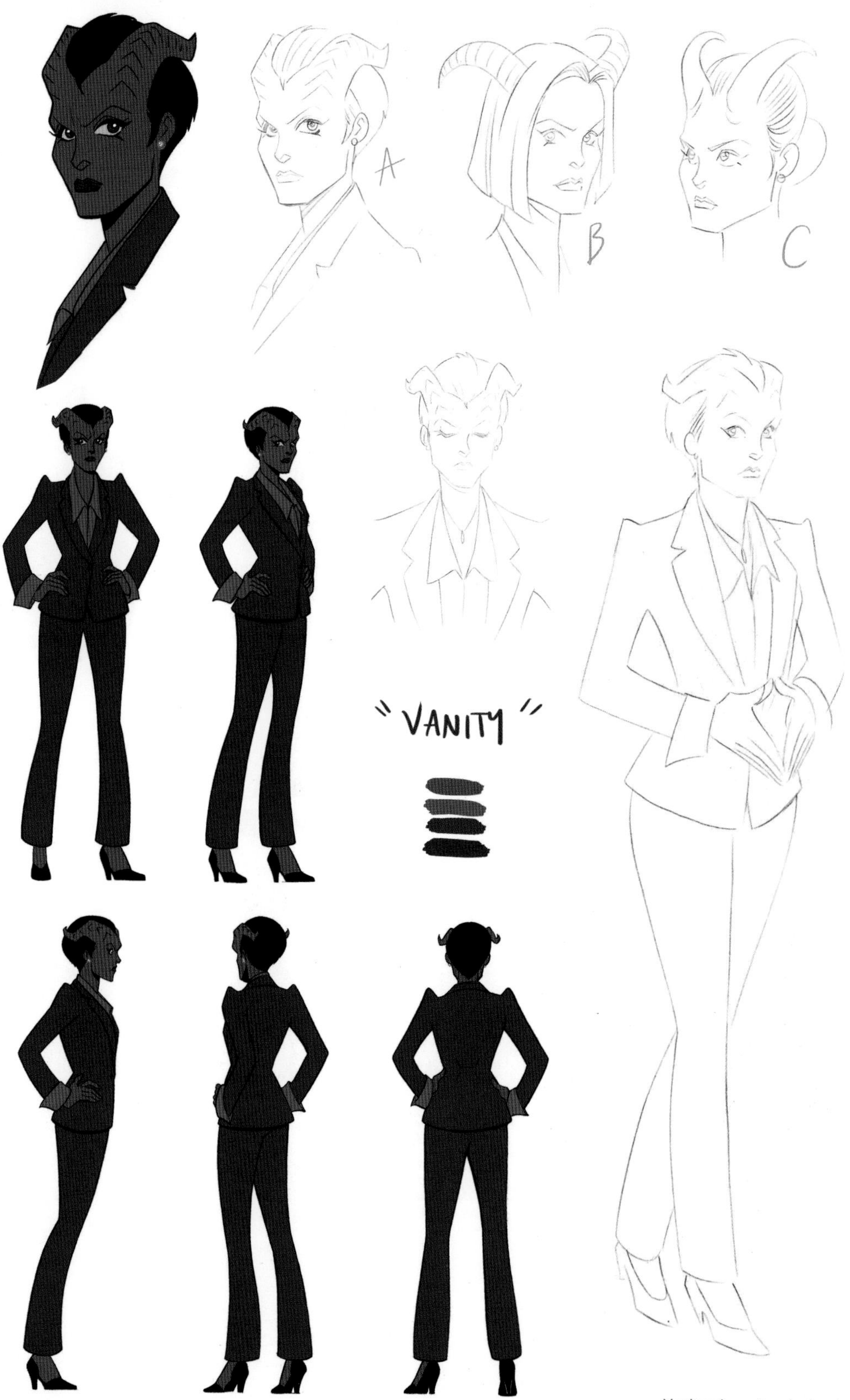
A
B
C
"VANITY"

Vanity character designs.

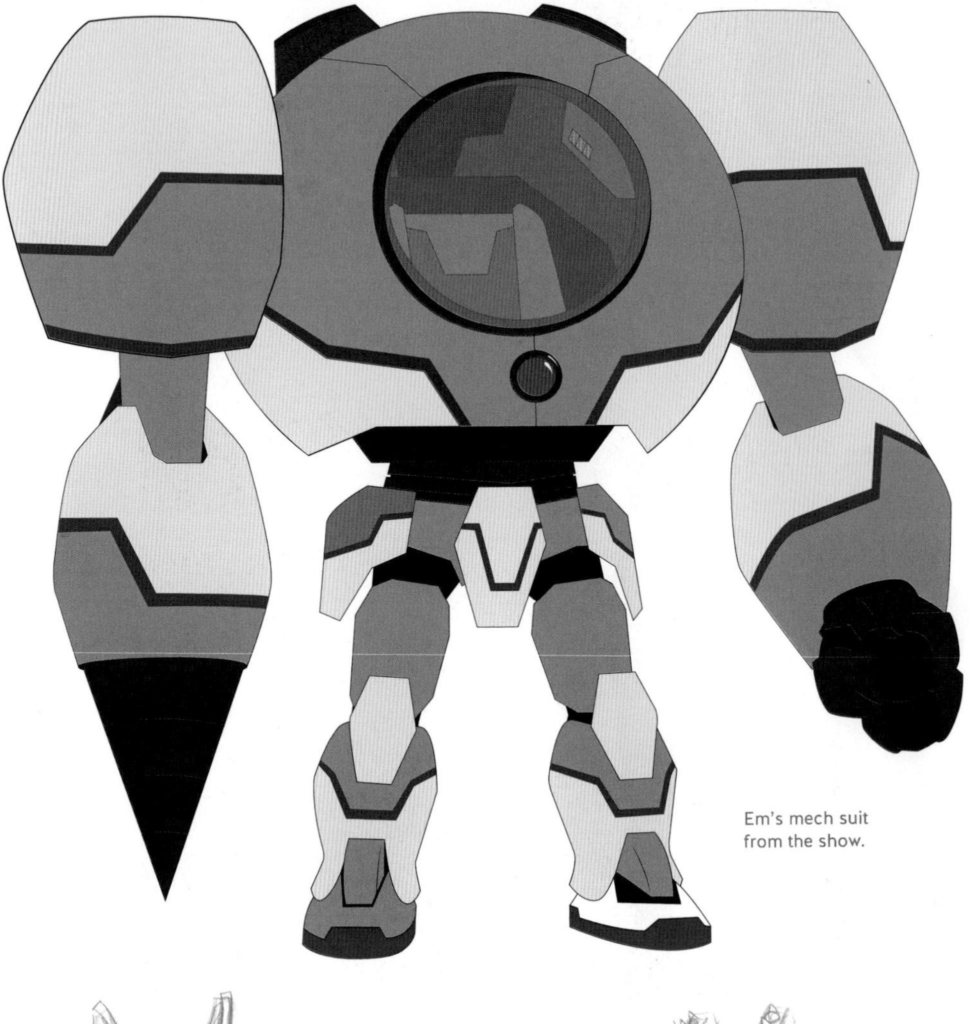

Em's mech suit from the show.

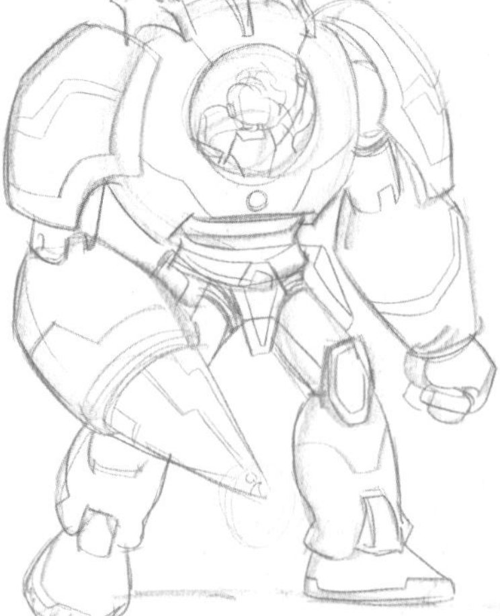

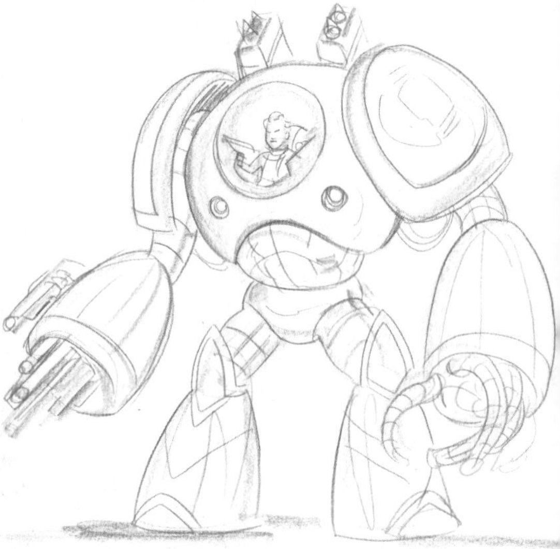

Mech suit designs by Megan Levens. Em's suit design is an upgraded version of her existing mech suit from the show.

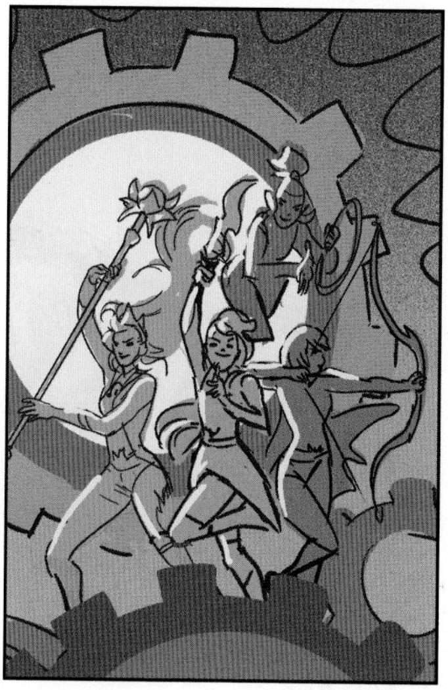
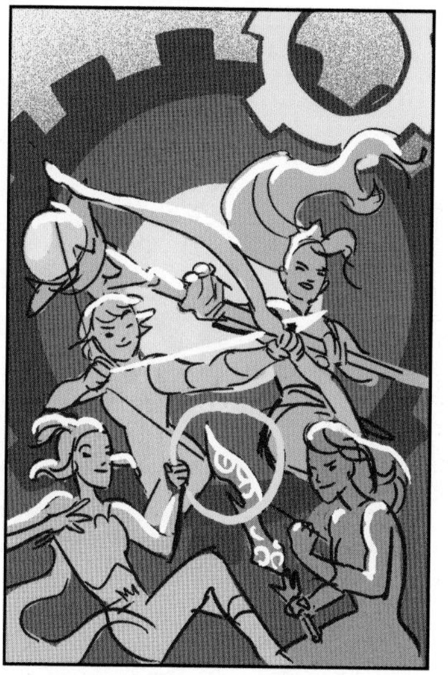
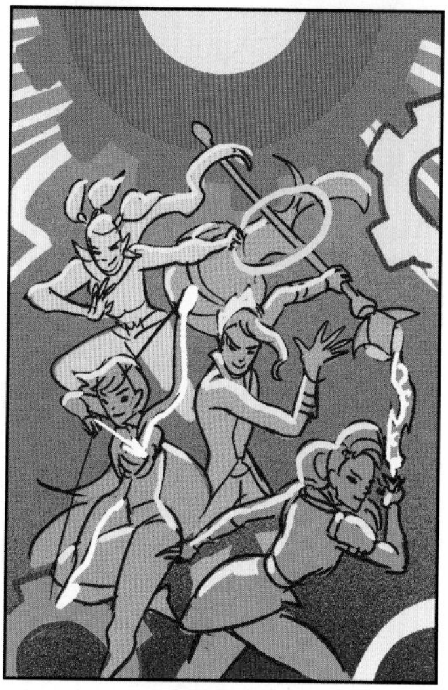
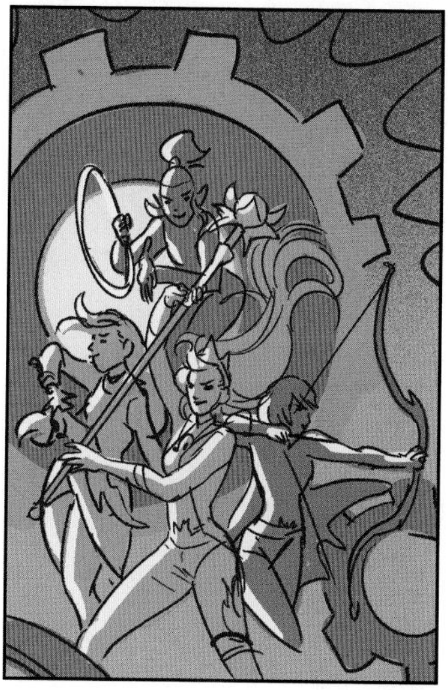
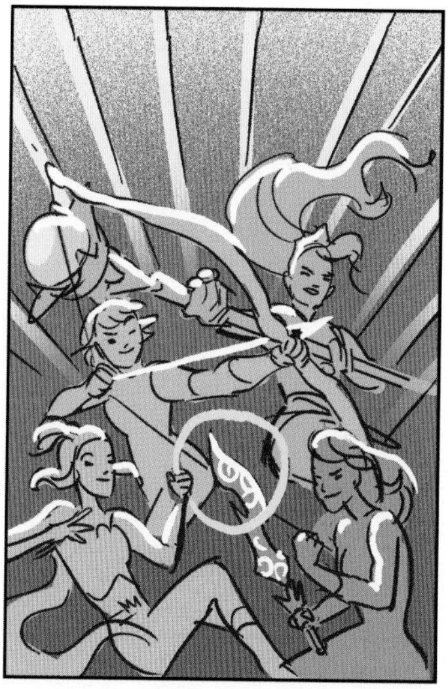
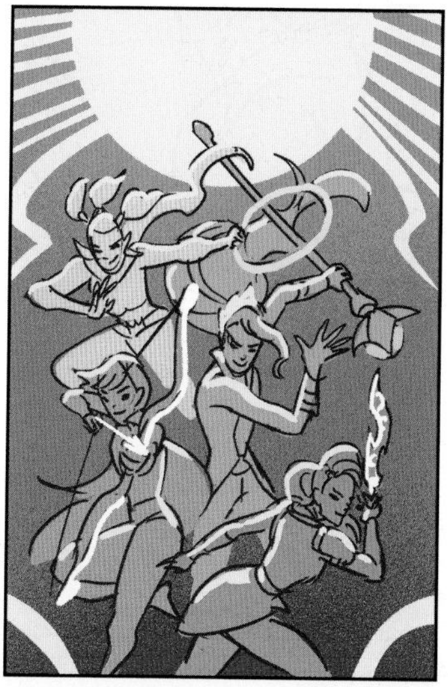

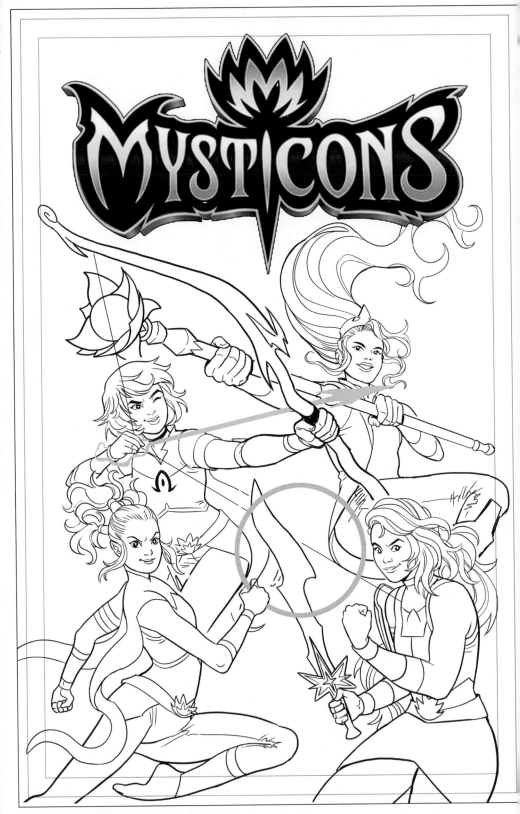

Cover concepts (previous page) and final pencils by Paulina Ganucheau.

THE ADVENTURE CONTINUES!

Enjoy novelizations and new adventures from Imprint
MAKE YOUR MARK

Available wherever books are sold!

MYSTICONS
BASED ON THE NEW HIT TV SHOW!
by SADIE CHESTERFIELD
QUEST FOR THE CODEX

MYSTICONS
AN ORIGINAL ADVENTURE FEATURING EM
THE SECRET OF THE FIFTH MYSTICON
LIZ MARSHAM

MYSTICONS
by SADIE CHESTERFIELD
BASED ON THE NEW HIT TV SHOW!
PROPHECY OF EVIL

THE STOLEN MAGIC

MYSTICONS
A BRAND-NEW ADVENTURE!
THE STOLEN MAGIC
LIZ MARSHAM

MYSTICONS SECRETS OF GEMINA

nelvana

GET IT ON Google play

Available on the App Store

Find Exclusive Mysticons Content on

YouTube

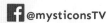

@mysticonsTV @mysticons @mysticonsTV MYSTICONS.COM

BOOKS THAT MIDDLE READERS WILL LOVE!

AVATAR: THE LAST AIRBENDER
Aang and friends' adventures continue right where the TV series left off, in these beautiful oversized hardcover collections, from *Airbender* creators Michael Dante DiMartino and Bryan Konietzko and Eisner and Harvey Award winner Gene Luen Yang!

The Promise ISBN 978-1-61655-074-5
The Search ISBN 978-1-61655-226-8
The Rift ISBN 978-1-61655-550-4
Smoke and Shadow ISBN 978-1-50670-013-7
North and South ISBN 978-1-50670-195-0
(Available October 2017)
$39.99 each

PLANTS VS. ZOMBIES
The hit video game continues its comic book invasion! Crazy Dave—the babbling-yet-brilliant inventor and top-notch neighborhood defender—helps his niece Patrice and young adventurer Nate Timely fend off a zombie invasion! Their only hope is a brave army of chomping, squashing, and pea-shooting plants!

Boxed Set #1: Lawnmageddon, Timepocalypse, Bully for You
ISBN 978-1-50670-043-4
Boxed Set #2: Grown Sweet Home, Garden Warfare,
The Art of Plants vs. Zombies
ISBN 978-1-50670-232-2
Boxed Set #3: Petal to the Metal, Boom Boom
Mushroom, Battle Extravagonzo
ISBN 978-1-50670-521-7 (Available October 2017)
$29.99 each

TREE MAIL
Mike Raicht, Brian Smith
Rudy—a determined frog—hopes to overcome the odds and land his dream job delivering mail to the other animals on Popomoko Island! Rudy always hops forward, no matter what obstacle seems to be in the way of his dreams!

ISBN 978-1-50670-096-0 **$12.99**

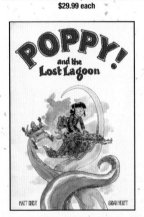

HOW TO TRAIN YOUR DRAGON: THE SERPENT'S HEIR
Picking up just after the events in *How to Train Your Dragon 2*, Hiccup, Astrid, and company are called upon to assist the people of an earthquake-plagued island. But their lives are imperiled by a madman and an incredible new dragon who even Toothless—the alpha dragon—may not be able to control!

ISBN 978-1-61655-931-1 **$10.99**

POPPY! AND THE LOST LAGOON
Matt Kindt, Brian Hurtt
At the age of ten, Poppy Pepperton is the greatest explorer since her grandfather Pappy! When a shrunken mummy head speaks, adventure calls Poppy and her sidekick/guardian, Colt Winchester, across the globe in search of an exotic fish—along the way discovering clues to what happened to Pappy all those years ago!

ISBN 978-1-61655-943-4 **$14.99**

SOUPY LEAVES HOME
Cecil Castellucci, Jose Pimienta
Two misfits with no place to call home take a train-hopping journey from the cold heartbreak of their eastern homes to the sunny promise of California in this Depression-era coming-of-age tale.

ISBN 978-1-61655-431-6 **$14.99**

DARKHORSE.COM
AVAILABLE AT YOUR LOCAL COMICS SHOP OR BOOKSTORE | TO FIND A COMICS SHOP IN YOUR AREA, VISIT COMICSHOPLOCATOR.COM
For more information or to order direct: On the web: DarkHorse.com •Email: mailorder@darkhorse.com •Phone: 1-800-862-0052 Mon.–Fri. 9 AM to 5 PM Pacific Time.
Avatar: The Last Airbender © Viacom International Inc. Plants vs. Zombies © Electronic Arts Inc. How to Train Your Dragon © DreamWorks Animation LLC. Tree Mail™ © Brian Smith and Noble Transmission Group, LLC.
Poppy!™ © Matt Kindt and Brian Hurtt. Soupy Leaves Home™ © Cecil Castellucci. Dark Horse Books® and the Dark Horse logo are registered trademarks of Dark Horse Comics, Inc. All rights reserved. (BL 6002 PI)

MORE TITLES YOU MIGHT ENJOY

ALENA
Kim W. Andersson
Since arriving at a snobbish boarding school, Alena's been harassed every day by the lacrosse team. But Alena's best friend Josephine is not going to accept that anymore. If Alena does not fight back, then she will take matters into her own hands. There's just one problem . . . Josephine has been dead for a year.

$17.99 | ISBN 978-1-50670-215-5

ASTRID: CULT OF THE VOLCANIC MOON
Kim W. Andersson
Formerly the Galactic Coalition's top recruit, the now-disgraced Astrid is offered a special mission from her old commander. She'll prove herself worthy of another chance at becoming a Galactic Peacekeeper . . . if she can survive.

$19.99 | ISBN 978-1-61655-690-7

BANDETTE
Paul Tobin, Colleen Coover
A costumed teen burglar by the *nome d'arte* of Bandette and her group of street urchins find equal fun in both skirting and aiding the law, in this enchanting, Eisner-nominated series!

$14.99 each
Volume 1: Presto! | ISBN 978-1-61655-279-4
Volume 2: Stealers, Keepers! | ISBN 978-1-61655-668-6
Volume 3: The House of the Green Mask | ISBN 978-1-50670-219-3

BOUNTY
Kurtis Wiebe, Mindy Lee
The Gadflies were the most wanted criminals in the galaxy. Now, with a bounty to match their reputation, the Gadflies are forced to abandon banditry for a career as bounty hunters . . . 'cause if you can't beat 'em, join 'em—then rob 'em blind!

$14.99 | ISBN 978-1-50670-044-1

HEART IN A BOX
Kelly Thompson, Meredith McClaren
In a moment of post-heartbreak weakness, Emma wishes her heart away and a mysterious stranger obliges. But emptiness is even worse than grief, and Emma sets out to collect the pieces of her heart and face the cost of recapturing it.

$14.99 | ISBN 978-1-61655-694-5

HENCHGIRL
Kristen Gudsnuk
Mary Posa hates her job. She works long hours for little pay, no insurance, and worst of all, no respect. Her coworkers are jerks, and her boss doesn't appreciate her. He's also a supervillain. Cursed with a conscience, Mary would give anything to be something other than a henchgirl.

$17.99 | ISBN 978-1-50670-144-8

DARK HORSE COMICS

DARKHORSE.COM AVAILABLE AT YOUR LOCAL COMICS SHOP OR BOOKSTORE • TO FIND A COMICS SHOP IN YOUR AREA, VISIT COMICSHOPLOCATOR.COM
For more information or to order direct: • On the web: DarkHorse.com • Email: mailorder@darkhorse.com • Phone: 1-800-862-0052 Mon.–Fri. 9 AM to 5 PM Pacific Time.

THE SECRET LOVES OF GEEK GIRLS
Hope Nicholson, Margaret Atwood, Mariko Tamaki, and more
The Secret Loves of Geek Girls is a nonfiction anthology mixing prose, comics, and illustrated stories on the lives and loves of an amazing cast of female creators.

$14.99 | ISBN 978-1-50670-099-1

THE SECRET LOVES OF GEEKS
Gerard Way, Dana Simpson, Hope Larson, and more
The follow-up to the smash hit *The Secret Loves of Geek Girls*, this brand new anthology features comic and prose stories from cartoonists and professional geeks about their most intimate, heartbreaking, and inspiring tales of love, sex, and dating. This volume includes creators of diverse genders, orientations, and cultural backgrounds.

$14.99 | ISBN 978-1-50670-473-9

MISFITS OF AVALON
Kel McDonald
Four misfit teens are reluctant recruits to save the mystical isle of Avalon. Magically empowered and directed by a talking dog, they must stop the rise of King Arthur. As they struggle to become a team, they're faced with the discovery that they may not be the good guys.

$14.99 each
Volume 1: The Queen of Air and Delinquency | ISBN 978-1-61655-538-2
Volume 2: The Ill-Made Guardian | ISBN 978-1-61655-748-5
Volume 3: The Future in the Wind | ISBN 978-1-61655-749-2

ZODIAC STARFORCE: BY THE POWER OF ASTRA
Kevin Panetta, Paulina Ganucheau
A group of teenage girls with magical powers have sworn to protect our planet against dark creatures. Known as the Zodiac Starforce, these high-school girls aren't just combating math tests—they're also battling monsters!

$12.99 | ISBN 978-1-61655-913-7

THE ADVENTURES OF SUPERHERO GIRL
Faith Erin Hicks
What if you can leap tall buildings and defeat alien monsters with your bare hands, but you buy your capes at secondhand stores and have a weakness for kittens? Faith Erin Hicks brings humor to the trials and tribulations of a young, female superhero, battling monsters both supernatural and mundane in an all-too-ordinary world.

$16.99 each | ISBN 978-1-61655-084-4
Expanded Edition | ISBN 978-1-50670-336-7

SPELL ON WHEELS
Kate Leth, Megan Levens, Marissa Louise
A road trip story. A magical revenge fantasy. A sisters-over-misters tale of three witches out to get back what was taken from them.

$14.99 | ISBN 978-1-50670-183-7

THE ONCE AND FUTURE QUEEN
Adam P. Knave, D.J. Kirkbride, Nick Brokenshire, Frank Cvetkovic
It's out with the old myths and in with the new as a nineteen-year-old chess prodigy pulls Excalibur from the stone and becomes queen. Now, magic, romance, Fae, Merlin, and more await her!

$14.99 | ISBN 978-1-50670-250-6

DARKHORSE.COM AVAILABLE AT YOUR LOCAL COMICS SHOP OR BOOKSTORE • TO FIND A COMICS SHOP IN YOUR AREA, VISIT COMICSHOPLOCATOR.COM
For more information or to order direct: • On the web: DarkHorse.com • Email: mailorder@darkhorse.com • Phone: 1-800-862-0052 Mon.–Fri. 9 AM to 5 PM Pacific Time.

2198231913936Q